# OUT OF FIRE AND ASH

## Jerry R. Stapleton

**DORRANCE**
PUBLISHING CO
EST. 1920
PITTSBURGH, PENNSYLVANIA 15238

Cover Portrait by Herbert Smagon

Dorrance Publishing Co
585 Alpha Drive
Pittsburgh, PA 15238
Visit our website at www.dorrancebookstore.com

ISBN: 978-1-6366-1370-3
EISBN: 978-1-6366-1947-7

# DEDICATION

For My Sons: Danny and Chris
For the Special Person in My Life: Amy
And especially in memory of my wife, Rhonda;
my brother, Mike; and my parents, Russ and Ingrid

*Out of Fire and Ash* is my first published book. There are many people who need to be thanked. First, I want to express my greatest appreciation to Danny, Chris, and Amy who supported and encouraged me in making my dream of this book a reality.

I would like to thank Kristina Banks and Mike Stephens whose input in building this story in a readable form was invaluable. Kristina is a former high school literature teacher in California. Mike is a childhood friend and former high school–college English teacher in addition to being an accomplished author.

I thank Stephen Jaffe and Susan Blakely for their consent in using Miss Blakely as one of my characters in the book.

I thank Daniel "Rudy" Ruettiger for allowing one of my main characters to be part of his Notre Dame experience.

Credit for historical information was provided from the book *The Firebombing of Dresden"* published by Charles River Editors. Additional historical information also provided by Wikipedia and The Anna Raccoon Archives blog: *The Rape of Dresden.*

The book cover is a reproduction of a portrait by German artist, Herbert Smagon.

And in memoriam, I would like to thank my parents for the inspiration of this story. I would also like to thank my wife, Rhonda, who taught me it was okay to dream and pursue those dreams. Also, my brother, Mike, who succumbed to cancer much to early in his life and would have enjoyed this story. Memories of Rhonda and Mike kept me going at times when I didn't think I could make it.

# CONTENTS

Chapter 1 — The Cemetery . . . . . . . . . . . . . . . . . . . . . . .1

Chapter 2 — Dresden . . . . . . . . . . . . . . . . . . . . . . . . . . .3

Chapter 3 — The Horror . . . . . . . . . . . . . . . . . . . . . . . .7

Chapter 4 — Destruction and Death . . . . . . . . . . . . . .13

Chapter 5 — The Soviets . . . . . . . . . . . . . . . . . . . . . . .17

Chapter 6 — Anna's Story . . . . . . . . . . . . . . . . . . . . . .23

Chapter 7 — The Escape and Arrival . . . . . . . . . . . . .27

Chapter 8 — New Life Begins . . . . . . . . . . . . . . . . . . .31

Chapter 9 — Marriage . . . . . . . . . . . . . . . . . . . . . . . . .35

Chapter 10 — Troublesome Years . . . . . . . . . . . . . . . .41

Chapter 11 — The Accident . . . . . . . . . . . . . . . . . . . .47

Chapter 12 — Kade Smith . . . . . . . . . . . . . . . . . . . . .49

Chapter 13 — Matt Kennedy . . . . . . . . . . . . . . . . . . .51

Chapter 14 — Notre Dame . . . . . . . . . . . . . . . . . . . .53

Chapter 15 — The Kennedy Foundation . . . . . . . . . . .57

Chapter 16 — Joseph Mason . . . . . . . . . . . . . . . . . . .61

Chapter 17 — Helping Hands Clinic . . . . . . . . . . . . .69

Chapter 18 — The Olympics . . . . . . . . . . . . . . . . . . .73

Chapter 19 — The Banquet . . . . . . . . . . . . . . . . . . . .77

Chapter 20 — The Reunion . . . . . . . . . . . . . . . . . . . .83

Chapter 21 — The Suitcase . . . . . . . . . . . . . . . . . . . .87

Chapter 22 — West Virginia . . . . . . . . . . . . . . . . . . .93

Chapter 23 — President Kennedy . . . . . . . . . . . . . . .97

Chapter 24 — Brothers . . . . . . . . . . . . . . . . . . . . . . .101

# Chapter 1

## THE CEMETERY

It was a cool, damp, humid day at the cemetery, typical for this time of the year in Savannah, Georgia in December. The cemetery was located just south of the city on the road to Tybee Island near Fort Pulaski. Reverend Joseph Mason, Mathew Kennedy, and Kade Smith walked through the 250-year-old cemetery, looking at the various grave markers trying to locate two headstones—both especially important to them.

It was the year 2010. Joe, Matt, and Kade were in their fifties. Joe, was the oldest of the three brothers; Kade, the youngest; and Matt, the driving force behind their expedition, was the middle brother.

They continued their walk through the sprawling cemetery of approximately ten acres. Although old, the cemetery was well kept and scenic. It was surrounded by oak trees draped in Spanish moss and bordered with a three-foot fence of carefully placed stacked river rock that stood the test of time.

They separated to expand their search since there were over a thousand graves, some unmarked or so old they were unreadable, some dating as far back as the late 1600s. Anxiety started to set in as the hours passed.

Matt shouted across the cemetery to Kade and Joe, "I don't believe they are buried here!"

"I believe they are!" Joe shouted, scanning the names to his right, and left, as he moved through the markers. The silence settled back in as they continued their search despite their dampening spirits.

Finally, Kade shouted, "I found them!"

Joe and Matt scurried over to Kade's location.

There they were. They found them. SFC Jake Castle, US Army—born 1927, died 1961. Anna Schmidt Castle—born 1927, died 1961. The inscription on the headstone read "Together Forever."

As they circled the graves, Joe, Matt, and Kade held hands, as Joe offered a prayer of thanksgiving and peace. They found their parents. With their search finished, they should have felt fulfilled. Yet, they left the cemetery wondering what their lives would have been had their parents survived that terrible accident.

With so many unanswered questions still buried in the past, their hopes turned to finding something in their parents' missing suitcase, found unopened at the orphanage. Who was Anna Schmidt? What was it like growing up in Germany and enduring World War II? What about her family? Who was Jake Castle? What about his heritage and family?

So many questions lingered—but they found their parents and that would sustain them for now… would give them peace for now. The answers to these questions were out there. Joe, Matt, and Kade pledged to find them.

# Chapter 2

## DRESDEN

History has not been kind or fair to Dresden, Germany; the world, distracted by so much violence elsewhere, paid little mind to the senseless destruction of the city during the latter days of World War II.

Located near the Czechoslovakia border on the Elbe River, 120 miles southeast of Berlin, Dresden was the capital of the German state of Saxony, often referred to as the "Florence of the Elbe," and regarded as the world's most beautiful city for its Baroque architecture, museums, and opera houses (many of these structures were over 200 years old prior to the destruction of the city). The glory of the city extended to the various parks and gardens that spread along the river and flourished throughout the downtown area, where an abundant variety of lindens, maples, birch, and the enormous Kaitz lime (one over 600 years old) graced the greenspaces. The city was a showplace of beauty and culture.

However, during the years of World War II, Dresden was a hospital town, and a city of refugees for eastern Germany. In the early weeks of 1945, the coldest winter in a century, Dresden was swollen with more than 700,000 refugees fleeing the advance of the Soviet army, most living in the city's main park, increasing the city's total population to over 1.2 million. Rural refugees who congregated down by the vast central railway station could be seen squatting in adjacent alleys relieving themselves because the lines for the lavatories were simply too long. This was not the kind of thing Dresdeners were used to witnessing.

By February 1945, the clear air in Dresden carried the smell of smoke. Although wartime coal supplies were never certain, the city's stoves and boilers were working against the morning cold. The snow was gone, but frosty silhouettes of breath still lingered in the chilled air. The elderly gentlemen with their hats and suits made their way to work in the banks and insurance companies near the Old Market maintaining a simulation of normalcy. Others moved more furtively through the narrow streets, some dodging past the cream-and-brown electric trams.

Extensive disruptions to schedules had become normal. Schools frequently closed, often to conserve fuel. Children were left to play winter games in the city's parks and in the wooded suburbs. Some classrooms had been converted into makeshift field hospitals for wounded soldiers brought back from the eastern front.

And while no German city remained isolated from Hitler's war machine, Dresden's contribution to the war effort was minimal compared with other German cities. Thus, residents of Dresden felt safe from the effects of war. They provided medical services, a haven for refugees, and a retreat for the exhausted German soldiers. It seemed unlikely that they would be a target for a major Allied air attack. Even with refugees and soldiers, Dresden seemed far from the war. Yet, there was an instinctive understanding that the world they knew was going to give way at any moment.

Even the Nazi leadership believed that the city was safe from attack, and there were numerous reasons for this belief: The Luftwaffe had not attacked Oxford (England); the Allies had too much love for the city to bomb it; Goering (head of the Luftwaffe) promised a raid on the city would never get through; the existence of English churches in Dresden would prevent the Allies from striking; the Allies would spare the city's cultural and architectural heritage this late in the war, and the Allies intended on making Dresden the new German capital after the war.

The Allied forces were closing in on Nazi Germany from the west. The Nazi's desperate counteroffensive against the Allies in Belgium's Ardennes Forest had ended in total failure. In the east, the Red army under Marshal George Zhuker captured East Prussia and reached the Oder River, less than fifty miles from Berlin and sixty miles from Dresden.

Many German civilians were starting to look at the prospect of a US occupation with a quiet degree of doubt due to the rapid advancing Red Army with less Nazi resistance and the slow progress of the Allies fighting their way through the heart of Germany from the west. However, as stories of rape and mutilation by the sociopathic Red Army made their way to Dresden, the idea of a Soviet conquest inspired real fear unlike their counterparts from the west where rumors of respect for the civilian population inspired hope for an Allied occupation.

A constant procession of tired horses moved through the city, carting young German soldiers and ordinance eastward, and weary refugee families westward.

Sometime in January of 1945, the Allies decided several large cities in Eastern Germany, that had escaped heavy bombing, should be subjected to "area bombing" or "blanket bombing" to wreak havoc on German morale and pressure Germany into surrendering sooner. The "Big Three" Allied leaders—Roosevelt, Churchill, and Stalin—agreed to continue their bombing campaign against eastern Germany in preparation for advancing Soviet forces. Stalin's senior commanders requested that the transport center of Dresden be targeted by American forces to hamper German movements to the eastern front. It was believed that bombing Dresden would disrupt important lines of communication that, otherwise, would have hindered the Soviet advance.

Thus, a British firebomb attack was recommended for Dresden under the orders of Prime Minister Churchill who was quoted saying,

"We will roast the Germans with our RAF bombers." Many historians believed this attack ordered by Churchill on Dresden was in retribution of the German Luftwaffe attack on the city of Coventry, England. During this attack, large parts of the city, over 100 acres, were damaged and the city's cathedral was mostly destroyed. The first planes, guided by electronic equipment, would drop both bombs and exploding incendiaries, and the resulting fires would give guidance to the attacks that would follow later. Destruction included factories, gas, sewer, water, and telephone lines, as well over 50,000 homes. This same protocol was followed by the RAF in the bombing of Dresden.

By this time, the once proud Luftwaffe, Germany's aerial warfare branch, was a skeleton of what they once were. There were no search lights, anti-aircraft guns or other countermeasures for an air attack. The flak guns had been removed to the eastern front and only decoys of papier-mâché remained in their place. The Allies ruled the skies over Europe. Therefore, while the terrified civilians of the German cities would see and hear the incoming bombers, the German Luftwaffe had been banned from night flights due to shortage of fuel.

Consequently, on February 13th, 1945, Dresden was alone and completely defenseless.

# Chapter 3

## THE HORROR

It was ten o'clock at night when the air-raid sirens started wailing. After a short period of silence, a wave of British Royal Air Force planes flew over Dresden dropping target flares. Anna, her mother, and grandmother saw the flares through the window of a friend's house filling the night sky with blinding light. Then, Anna felt the throb of hundreds of heavy bombers that filled the air, getting nearer and louder by the second. She saw the flares still falling and exploding when the initial stream flew over, dropping thousands of incendiaries, laced with napalm, along with high explosive bombs blowing off roofs, windows, and doors of structures, lighting up the sky and city. Anna saw the sky change from a bright white to a dull red that danced before dying. Anna wanted to scream, "Where was the Luftwaffe?' But she knew it was too late.

Seventeen-year-old Anna Schmidt, her mother, and grandmother, with unrelenting fear, hurried to their apartment building located near the banks of the Elbe River. As they raced toward the building, Anna saw a woman carrying a bundle in her arms. It was a baby. The woman ran, she fell, and the child flew in an arc into the fire.

Before Anna and her mother reached the safety of their apartment home, she saw the horror of other people in front of her. They screamed and gestured with their hands, and then—she saw them simply drop to the ground. They fainted—then burned to cinders. Insane fear overcame Anna. She repeatedly told her mother as they ran, "I don't want to burn to death."

The streets Anna knew so well were difficult to maneuver. Everything was in flames. Even the roads became burning rivers of bubbling and hissing tar. Anna observed a group of people that tried to run from the flames across a road "got stuck," trapped in the bubbling mass of molten tar. One by one she saw them fall through sheer exhaustion and then the fiery winds consumed them. They collapsed, burst into flames, and then simply exploded. As if the Devil himself decided their torments were not sufficient above the wind's howl, with the inferno's roar she heard the interminable agonized screams of the victims being roasted alive.

Anna found a few survivors as they made their way home. Utter panic ensued all around them as horses reared and ran into the crowd. Lions and tigers, that escaped from the broken enclosures of the zoo, charged into the terrified crowds. Huge snakes slithered between the feet of the fleeing. Anna saw hospital trains that pulled out of the burning station filled with wounded soldiers from the eastern front and, in the process, severed limbs from young children underneath who had sought cover from the bombs.

The noise of the planes died down and people started to appear from the few houses still intact. Survivors clawed their way through mounds of rubble an hour before what had been their homes. The first thing that hit Anna on her way to the apartment was the heat. Wherever she turned, she was confronted with flames, smoke and dust and blocks of debris falling from the sky. Anna, her mother, and grandmother stumbled along the remains of a wide avenue, flanked by fires and mountains of red-hot wreckage.

Anna, her mother, and grandmother made it to their apartment building. They scurried to the cellar ill-prepared for more bombs. Fear consumed them.

Anna's apartment building was converted from an established, centuries old castle known as the Dresden Castle or Royal Palace, one of the oldest buildings in Dresden built around 1200. It was modernized in 1914 with in-floor heating and electric lights. It was converted to State supported apartments prior to World War II. As with most castles, it was well insulated with stone and thick walls. However, the castle was reduced to a roofless shell. The basement became a sanctuary for the residents and other survivors.

The castle, located on the banks of the Elbe River, prevented the structure from being destroyed from the bombs and 100-mile-per-hour winds heated to 1,100 degrees. Thousands of others suffocated in cellars throughout the city as the oxygen was sucked out of the bunkers and pulled toward the blaze to feed the flames if they were not already burned alive by the phosphorus bombs. Thousands more were hurled into the air like rag dolls and sucked by the ferocious winds right into the inferno. The air suction was so strong it uprooted trees and lifted roofs from houses miles away.

Anna, her mother, and grandmother were safe for the time being, but the exploding bombs and the screams of the people outside could be heard even in the remote parts of the castle's cellar. Then, Anna felt this eerie calm for the next two hours. They survived but was this the end? Would there be more bombing? Anna, her mother, and grandmother did not want to leave the sanctity of the basement. They did not want to see the horror of the destruction of their proud city. However, they felt more destruction was to come.

Then, the second wave started. Some 800 British aircraft dropped more than 1,400 tons of high-explosive bombs and more than 1,100 tons of incendiary devices creating a great firestorm. Anna knew it would catch the fire brigade and rescue workers in the open. Many more civilians died from the firestorm.

Within fifteen minutes huge clouds of smoke and flame preceded the enormous pull as air rushed into the vacuum. Cellars and other shelters were meager protection against the firestorm that blew poisonous air heated to 1,100 degrees Fahrenheit across the city at hurricane-like speed.

The next day, more than 300 US bombers bombed Dresden's bridges and transportation facilities, killing thousands more. Anna saw the Allies's planes even though they were thousands of feet up, but she could see their outlines reflected in the glow. As their bombs fell, Anna realized this raid was nothing like the last one. These bombs were so big that you could see them in the sky. Even the phosphorous bombs were different—four-ton objects that exploded on the ground, running along the ground, incinerating anything within a radius of 200 feet. Raining down with these came more blockbusters, each one ten tons this time.

The railway yards were the targets of the Americans. Those that escaped before were now getting the same treatment. Although the Americans dropped much less destructive bombs than the British, many more were killed. Anna could feel the heat from the inferno created by the firebombs even through the well-insulated walls of the basement. Her body shook as the ground vibrated from the conventional bombs. And if this was not enough, another terror made its presence felt—the air being drawn in to feed the inferno out of their cellar.

Anna, her mother, and grandmother decided to leave the basement for air and safety of the Elba River as the fires intensified drawing oxygen from the smoke-filled air. Anna was horrified. Those that escaped to the safety of the Elbe riverbanks, mostly women and children, became victims of low flying fighter planes. Anna, her mother, and grandmother quickly returned to the castle basement as they were fired upon by squadron of fighter planes. Anna felt a sharp pain in her leg but kept running to the safety of the castle basement. They safely reached the basement as Anna discovered a wound in her leg believed to be a cut. She tore some cloth and tightly wrapped it to slow the bleeding.

Anna asked her mother, "Why did the planes shoot women and children? What kind of war is this?"

"Those are questions I will never be able to answer," replied Anna's mother.

The bombing stopped. The roar of the fires could still be heard. Anna, her mother, and grandmother decided to stay until morning knowing Dresden will never be the same.

# Chapter 4

# DEATH AND DESTRUCTION

Anna, her mother, and grandmother saw the horrific destruction and loss of life the days following the bombing. The smell was intolerable with decaying, burning corpses lining the streets. Children under the age of three or four had simply melted.

Between two to three hundred thousand of the more than one million residents and refugees, mostly women and children, lost their life. By comparison, Hiroshima's atomic bomb casualties totaled 71,879. No one is sure of the losses because many were liquefied as a jellied mass into the asphalt of the roads or were left in piles of ash. Undocumented refugees could not be accounted for that just evaporated from the horrific heat and destruction. More than 13 square miles of Dresden lay in smoldering ruins. Six of seven homes had been destroyed along with 72 schools, 22 hospitals, 19 churches, 5 theaters, and 31 department stores.

Along the main street through Dresden, Anna saw clean-up crews piling 50 to 100 bodies approximately ten feet high on railroad ties used as grids—soldiers, young and old women, boys in short pants, girls with braids, Red Cross nurses, babies. These mounds of people could be seen at every intersection as far as she could see.

A few days later, Anna and her mother returned to the streets looking for food and water. She saw and smelled the burning bodies at the various intersections.

Anna asked a local worker, "Why are you burning the dead?"

"To prevent the spread of disease. We don't have the resources to bury all these people."

While all of Germany shivered for lack of fuel, these pyres burned day and night. Some of the corpses were so brittle that they crumbled into clouds of ash and dried flesh. Identifiable parts of these corpses were placed into sacks. There were no real, complete bodies, only bones and scorched articles of clothing matted together or stuck together by a sort of jelly. There was no flesh visible, just a glutinous mass of solidified fat and bones.

Anna will never forget the sight and smell of the bodies burning on the streets as far as she could see. It is a horror that will remain burned in her memory and, like Dresden's fires, impossible to extinguish.

Later in the week, Anna described the horror to a German Information Officer from Berlin, "And the town was burning. There was a glowing fire, darkness at the same time. It was indescribable— so cruel. A woman and her daughter burned. My friend lived next door. There were about twenty children living there altogether. They were burned alive. Several of the dead were naked. They tore off their clothes because they were on fire. I was frozen with horror. Other survivors trying to escape were blackened from the smoke and fire."

A friend of Anna's mother, Rudolph Eichner, also shared his account of the bombing to the information officer, "There were no warning sirens. We were completely surprised and rushed back down to the cellars of the hospital. But these quickly became hopelessly overcrowded with people who could no longer find shelter in their own burning buildings. The crush was unbearable; we were so tight you could not fall over. Apart from the fire risk, it was becoming increasingly impossible to breathe in the cellar because the air was being pulled out by the increasing strength of the blaze. We could not stand up. We were on all fours, crawling. The wind was full of sparks and carrying bits of blazing furniture, debris and burning bits of bodies. There were charred bodies everywhere. The experience of the bombing was far worse than being on the Russian front, where I was a frontline machine gunner."

Anna also heard Gotz Bergander, a German soldier and citizen, describe his account of the devastation. "There was an indescribable roar in the air, the fire. The thundering fire reminded me of the biblical catastrophes I had heard about in my education in the humanities. I was aghast. I cannot describe seeing the city burn in any other way. The color had changed as well. It was no longer pinkish-red. The fire had become a furious white and yellow, and the sky was just one massive mountain of cloud. The blaze roared, with intermittent blasts of either delayed-action bombs or unexploded bombs, which were engulfed by the flames."

Anna, her mother, and grandmother survived the following days, locating food and water with the help of other survivors. Even in those times there was red cabbage and fried potatoes. There could be scant cause for unhappiness if one "could still enjoy fried potatoes though I still miss potato soup and potato dumplings," said Anna.

Anna ran into her childhood friend, Monika, while scavenging for food. Monika and her family also survived the bombing.

# Chapter 5

## THE SOVIETS

A few weeks after the city was decimated, Anna saw the Soviet soldiers come and occupy what was left of Dresden. The underlying fears of brutality and unstoppable violence were compounded by other profound anxieties.

The soldiers were brutal. They sought revenge for Operation Barbarossa, Hitler's invasion of the USSR, the death of one million Soviet soldiers and civilians in Leningrad. It was the defenseless women, girls, and even elderly ladies who were to pay in pain and death for the crimes of their male compatriots. Anyone between the ages of 8 and 70 were in danger.

Officially rape was a crime in the Red Army, but Stalin explicitly condoned it as a method of rewarding the soldiers and terrorizing German civilians. He said, "We lecture our soldiers too much; let them have their initiative." Those German men who objected or tried to protect the ladies were shot.

Anna saw her friend, Monika, on the street one day. Monika was a "streetwise" girl, accustomed to navigating the city unseen. Monika told Anna she witnessed the horror of the Soviet soldiers during recent excursions.

"I saw men shot on the spot. Women, without exception, gang raped, girls as young as eight years old as well as old women in their eighties. Pregnant women too. Women who resisting had their throats cut or were shot. I saw women murdered after being gang raped. My fifteen-year-old cousin was raped seven times. My twenty-six-year-old aunt was raped fifteen times. I saw a Soviet Officer herding woman into what they thought was the safety of a Cathedral. They were locked inside as Soviet soldiers entered raping all the women through the night, some more than thirty times."

Monika assured Anna she would come by periodically to check on her, her mother, and grandmother. "Stay off the streets. I will bring you food and water when I can."

Monika left. Anna was so envious of her. Anna was intelligent and athletic, but Monika was street-smart, bold, and daring.

Anna, her mother, and grandmother were in the basement of their apartment building when four Soviet soldiers came in the evening. They entered the basement, searching for items, destroying what they did not steal. Anna, her mother (age 39) and grandmother (age 62), were taken to the street along with their mattresses. Anna, seventeen and a virgin, with her mother and grandmother, were brutally raped and sodomized. Anna's grandmother did not survive, succumbing to her injuries from the brutal and ruthless attack.

Following the attack, three of the four soldiers gathered several local men from the street and made them watch while Anna was tied to a wagon wheel, naked, brutalized by the Soviet soldiers again. Then the men were lined up and shot eliminating witnesses to the atrocity. The soldiers took Anna's grandmother along with the men to a nearby bomb crater. They placed and buried the bodies in the crater never to be seen again.

Anna and her mother returned to what was left of their living area in the basement, battered and bruised, permanently damaged both physically and psychologically. They knew the soldiers would come again especially for Anna.

A few days later, the four Soviet soldiers returned looking for Anna and her mother. They entered the apartment prepared to brutalize them again. However, a Soviet sergeant appeared and ordered the soldiers away, warning them not to return.

"My name is Mikhail Petrov," he told Anna and her mother. "I assure you they will not return, or I will have them shot. I do not want to be a party to their crimes or indulge in their indiscretions."

Mikhail told Anna he was from Leningrad, formerly St. Petersburg. He lost his family—wife and two daughters—to the Germans in their invasion of Russia along with many other Russian citizens. He despised Hitler and the German soldiers but did not blame the German people for the atrocities. He did not agree with Stalin's edict of brutalizing German civilians in retribution of lost Russian lives in Leningrad.

Sergeant Petrov warned Anna there are others over whom he had no authority or control. He suggested they stay hidden and off the streets. Anna cried and thanked the sergeant as he left.

Sergeant Petrov returned to his barracks on the outskirts of Dresden. The four soldiers who were there, approached him and asked to speak in private. They all stepped outside of the barracks. The lead soldier made it clear he did not like the interference in their business with the general German population. If he was not careful, he may invite a stray bullet from an enemy gun.

Petrov told the soldiers, "If that stray bullet misses me, I assure you the four bullets in my gun will find a home in each of you. You know the Germans are poor shots anyway and I am sure you are aware of my background and accomplishments in Leningrad. I order you to stay away from the castle. Do not test me!"

The four soldiers stayed away—for the time being.

Mikhail Petrov was born in 1910 in St. Petersburg (name changed to Leningrad in 1924), the son of a factory worker. He always wanted to join the military as a child. He joined the Soviet Army at the age of eighteen. He admired Joseph Stalin and was committed to his regime.

Two years later, in the spring of 1930, he met and married Natasha. The following four years Natasha gave birth to two beautiful girls, Katrina and Zarya.

World War II started in 1939 with Hitler's eyes on Russia. The German Army's campaign against Leningrad started in September 1941, and it lasted until January 1944. Fighting was brutal with the loss of over one million Leningrad women, children, men, and Soviet soldiers.

Mikhail was in the infantry fighting the Nazi's on the front lines. He developed a reputation as an excellent marksman. He was summoned by his commanding officer to discuss a reassignment of duties to Leningrad.

Mikhail arrived at the headquarters building and was introduced to General Nikita Khrushchev. Khrushchev was impressed with Mikhail's service and reputation with a rifle. He promoted Mikhail to sergeant and reassigned him to sniper duty. He was given permission to roam Leningrad, set up and kill as many German officers or SS troops as possible. He was remarkably successful in his new duties killing forty-seven of the enemy. He received the highest award of the Soviet Union for heroism, the Honor of the Soviet Union medallion, a five-point gold star at the end of a red ribbon.

Natasha, Katerina, and Zarya were relatively safe in a protected area of Leningrad. Late in 1943, the Nazis pushed through Leningrad capturing Natasha and her children along with many other residents in the area. Mikhail vacated his post and ran back to their home in northern Leningrad when he heard the news about the Nazi capture of this part of Leningrad.

Mikhail found his home charred from fire, but he was still able to enter. Mikhail found his family—no clothes, brutally raped, shot, then butchered. Mikhail fainted when he found them. They were tortured before succumbing to their wounds.

Neighboring soldiers found Mikhail and carried him to the nearest hospital tent. He woke up, became belligerent and violent. The doctors sedated him. The doctors told his commanding officer it would be some time before he would return to normal, if ever. They felt it best to have him reassigned to noncombat duty for the duration of the war. Mikhail was reassigned to a division primarily charged with holding captured towns or cities until reinforcements could arrive.

Mikhail struggled with his loss for many months. He made many enemies under his new command as he had disdain for troops that engaged in Stalin's retribution tactics. He believed this made the Soviet soldiers as despicable as the Nazi's.

Mikhail desperately wanted the war to end. He was tired of all the death and horror he witnessed, memories that will haunt him for the rest of his life.

# Chapter 6

## ANNA'S STORY

Anna was born in the summer of 1927 to Marie and Hans Schmidt. She grew up an only child. Marie was a stay-at-home mom and Hans worked for the railroad. Anna was athletic and quite intelligent, proven by her consistent and exceptional grades in school. She ran track and was an outstanding swimmer. She earned numerous medals for her achievements.

Hans was an accountant for the local office of a major railroad company based in Dresden. An unscheduled audit of the financial records of the company found funds missing or unaccounted for. Hans was accused and subsequently arrested in 1933 for embezzlement of company funds. He was released until his trial.

Hans wanted to avoid the publicity of a trial and imprisonment, especially for his wife and Anna. Just before the trial, Hans committed suicide at the age of thirty-two by placing his head in a gas oven and slowly suffocated. The consequence of this event resulted in an unfortunate turn for Anna.

Following the death of Hans, German Social Services removed eight-year-old Anna from her home despite her mother's pleading. Anna was placed in a group home for girls. This is where she met Monika who would become her lifelong friend.

After the death of Hans, Marie took a job at the local sewing machine manufacturing plant to find income and stability in her life while trying to get Anna back. Singer Sewing Machines started in 1903 and sold their product worldwide.

When Anna turned thirteen, Marie applied to have Anna returned to her. Her request was granted.

Anna continued to maintain her friendship with Monika although no longer at the group home.

Adolf Hitler traveled to Dresden during the summer of 1940 to inspect a section of the newly created autobahn highway system. A parade was held in his honor. Anna asked her mother if she could see the parade and Hitler. She agreed.

As Hitler traveled down the streets of Dresden, he left his vehicle, and shook hands with the crowd as he walked along the street. Thirteen-year-old Anna shook Hitler's hand as he passed. She felt honored although the people of Dresden were not aware of the horrors of the war and plight of the Jewish people in the concentration camps. Over 7,000 Jews were removed from Dresden and transported to nearby Auschwitz or Dachau.

Unknown to Anna, a local news photographer took a picture of Hitler shaking her hand. The photographer asked where she lived. Anna told him. He told Anna that he would be by in a few days and give her a copy of the photograph but needed permission from her mother to publish it in the Berlin newspaper. This excited Anna.

The photographer arrived at Anna's apartment two days later. He met Anna's mother. She agreed to allow the photograph to be published. He handed Anna a copy of the picture. She was thrilled to have a copy of a published picture in Berlin's largest newspaper of her and Hitler.

Between 1941 and late 1944, as the war raged on, things became increasingly difficult for Anna and her mother. Supplies, food, and other necessities became increasingly scarce. Refugees and wounded soldiers poured in from the east fleeing the oncoming Soviet war machine. Additionally, the worst winter Dresden had seen in more than a generation arrived late 1944 – early 1945, adding misery to an already emotionally and physically strained population.

Then, in February 1945, the bombing started.

# Chapter 7

# THE ESCAPE AND ARRIVAL

World War II ended in Europe with Germany surrendering on May 7, 1945. The Allies and Soviets divided Germany into two countries, East Germany and West Germany, a result of an agreement made early 1945 as the war was winding down.

East Germany was controlled by the Communists and West Germany by the Allies. Dresden became part of Communist East Germany. Berlin was also geographically divided east and west between the Communists and Allies with the Allies controlling the western half.

The terror in Dresden did not stop with Germany's surrender. Although killing civilians and raping women subsided substantially, life in Dresden was unbearable as the Soviets continued to brutalize the German citizens.

Monika and Anna continued to see each other as their friendship thrived after leaving the group home. Monika was a troubled child but also a free spirit. She was a rebel. She resisted authority, both legal and at home. Her disobedience got her placed in the group home by her parents. It did not help her and was counterproductive.

Monika lived in the southwest part of Dresden. She had just a few months previously completed an apprenticeship that in peacetime might not have been available to her. She now had a full-time position in the local brewery, one of many breweries that thrived around the city. Beer sold as well in peacetime as in war.

Monika was tall and thin for her age but not particularly attractive. She smoked cigarettes and engaged in other vices certainly frowned upon in a conservative time and city such as Dresden. She was volatile, explosive, and emotional. But she was a scavenger and a survivor.

Monika could physically challenge any boy her age. She was mean when she had to be but could be a valued friend if one gained her confidence. Although not "book" smart, she was "foxy" or street-smart. She was a risk-taker.

Anna saw Monika differently. Anna wanted to be Monika's friend. But Monika saw something different in Anna too. Monika was never a happy person and envied Anna. Anna made Monika feel good about herself. They became fast friends although they had extreme opposite personalities.

During the Spring of 1946, Monika approached Anna with the idea of escaping to West Germany. Anna did not want to leave her mother. She was also afraid of being caught and imprisoned or worse. Anna knew about the barriers, guards and dogs patrolling the border. She refused to leave. Monika understood but told Anna, "One must be prepared to take risk—or else one is never really alive."

A few days later, the four Soviet soldiers that previously assaulted Anna and her mother a year earlier, paid Anna a visit. They told Anna their sergeant was reassigned, and they would be back later to get "reacquainted." A terrified Anna immediately sought out Monika.

Anna saw Monika later that day. Anna told Monika she was ready to go to West Germany. The two eighteen-year-old girls planned to leave that night on a 200-mile journey to the West German border. They gathered some clothes, a few supplies, and some food. They planned to leave Dresden at midnight. Monika assured her she knew a route not well traveled that would take them through the Thuringia Forest to Meiningen near the border.

Midnight came. They met at the western edge of the city near the river and started their journey. Anna regretted leaving her mother but knew she was too old, frail, and worn out to travel. She hoped her mother would forgive her and survive the unbearable conditions.

Monika and Anna traveled along a dirt road through the difficult Thuringia Forest. Thuringia Forest was considered southwest Germany's "Black Forest." The Black Forest received its name from the fifty square miles of dense, seasoned trees so thick the sun's rays are blocked, causing midday to become night. Rumors and tales of hikers becoming lost and never found were rampant.

Anna and Monika received help along the way from sympathetic residents and other travelers. Occasionally they encountered Soviet troops on the road. Anna and Monika would leave the road and hide until they passed. They knew their Soviet issued identification cards would bring suspicion and, if caught, they would be returned to Dresden.

They arrived in Meiningen after ten days on the road. Locals told them the border was approximately ten miles away but heavily guarded with troops and dogs. Also, there were coils of razor wire in places where the terrain was suitable for travel.

One of the local citizens showed them a map of a path to the border through a heavily wooded area with difficult terrain. Anna and Monika elected to take this route.

They started out early the next morning. They reached the border without incident but heard gunfire and barking dogs in the distance. They became quite concerned and quietly wondered if they made the right decision. Anna was most concerned, but Monika was confident, but both knew they made the right decision.

Anna and Monika crossed the border to West Germany and spotted a farmhouse on the horizon. They approached the farmhouse and met an elderly couple, Mr. and Mrs. Hoffmeier. The Hoffmeiers were delightful people and anxious to help the young girls.

Anna and Monika stayed with the Hoffmeiers for a few days. Mr. Hoffmeier offered to drive them to Frankfurt, the location of a refugee and placement camp. They accepted the offer and rode approximately sixty miles to Frankfurt. The camp was located just outside the city limits.

They thanked Hoffmeier with tears of sadness and happiness. They made it, but Anna still wondered about her mother.

Anna and Monika registered with an army marshal at the camp and gave him their background information. Anna and Monika spoke good English, a byproduct of school where it was mandatory to take English as a subject.

The marshal was impressed with their command of the English language and indicated there was an increasing need for bilingual workers in Frankfurt. They both applied for civil service work permits.

After a few days in the camp, they were introduced to a US Army Captain. He indicated jobs were available as housekeepers for stationed officers in Frankfurt. Both accepted and were placed.

Anna became an employee of Colonel Ray Stevens. Colonel Stevens and his wife were very pleasant and easy to work for. Special quarters were provided for Anna. After a few weeks, Anna lost contact with Monika. In the months that followed, Anna heard Monika fell on hard times and became a prostitute.

Several years passed. All was going well with Anna. She was comfortable in her new life and happy but still missed her mother.

# Chapter 8

## NEW LIFE BEGINS

Anna was doing well in her new surroundings and working for Colonel Stevens. She finally located Monika. They continued to share their experiences. Anna started corresponding with her mother. Her mother was happy that some form of normalcy returned to Dresden even though life under Communist rule was difficult. Her mother said they started rebuilding Dresden, but Anna knew it would never be as it was before.

Anna continued her duties with Colonel Stevens and his family. Colonel Stevens's children loved her. She was considered part of the family.

Ray Stevens was born 1918 in Columbus, Georgia. His father was an officer stationed at Camp Benning renamed Fort Benning in later years. Ray's father was a decorated veteran of World War I.

Ray graduated from Columbus High School and earned an academic scholarship to West Point Academy in 1935. He graduated from West Point in 1939 obtaining the rank of Lieutenant. After graduation, Lt. Stevens was assigned to Schofield Barrack near Pearl Harbor and assigned to the Intelligence Unit. While in Hawaii, Lt. Stevens married the daughter of a local farmer. His wife's family had a long history on the island of Maui. He fathered two girls the following four years.

In the fall of 1941, Lieutenant Stevens suspected a surprise Japanese attack on a US site was imminent within the coming months. Intelligence information led them to believe it would be Guam or the Philippines. Stevens tried to convince his superiors it could be Pearl Harbor. His commanding officers thought Hawaii was too far from Japan to sustain an attack. December 7 proved his commanding officers were wrong. Lt. Stevens was promoted to Major for his diligent and tireless work in providing substantial information on Japanese movements. Major Stevens was promoted to Colonel in June 1945 and reassigned to Germany to command the division assigned to Frankfurt.

Anna was invited to Colonel Stevens's birthday party at the Officers Club at the Army's base. It was 1948. Anna just turned twenty-one years old. She was apprehensive about the party being in a room full of uniformed military men as her nightmares of that night in Dresden continued. She was not sure about attending but committed to go.

Anna rode to the Officers Club with Colonel Stevens and his family. Other German ladies were in attendance. She felt at ease. Many of the German ladies were refugees from Eastern Germany too, leaving family and friends behind to avoid the horrors of the Soviets and to find a better life.

A young sergeant approached Anna and started a conversation. He introduced himself—Jake Castle—from the mountains of West Virginia. He was attached to Colonel Stevens's division and was invited to his birthday party too.

Anna thought Jake was good-looking and athletic. Surprisingly, Anna's English and grammar were far superior to Jake's even though she spoke with a heavy accent. But Jake had a magnetic personality and Anna was drawn to him. She told Jake about how she escaped from East Germany with her friend, Monika. Jake told her he joined the Army in 1946 to also escape—West Virginia.

"If I stayed, I would either be a coal miner or a farmer. There were no jobs. My father was a poor farmer, and my brother was a coal miner with lung disease from inhaling coal dust," explained Jake.

After a lengthy conversation, Jake felt comfortable and asked Anna if she would be interested in a date. She agreed. They settled on the following Saturday.

Jake picked up Anna at Colonel Stevens's house Saturday. They went to the local NCO club where they met some of Jake's friends. They enjoyed the evening. Anna relished meeting new people, some military, and some German. They danced and drank through the night. Jake returned Anna home. The evening was a success.

Jake Castle was born in the fall of 1927 in southwest West Virginia near the Big Sandy River. His grandmother was the daughter of William Anderson Hatfield, also known as "Devil Anse," of the infamous Hatfields and McCoys feud. Jake always avoided conversations regarding the feud. He was not proud of his family's heritage.

Many family members of the Hatfields and McCoys lost their lives during the 1870s. The feud began when Asa Harmon McCoy was murdered by a militia group headed by Devil Anse Hatfield. It became deadly when Randolph McCoy accused Floyd Hatfield of stealing one of his pigs. It became increasingly complicated and more violent when a Hatfield son married a McCoy daughter.

Settling the feud or bringing those involved to justice was complicated. Enforcing the law was difficult since the McCoys lived in Kentucky and the Hatfields lived in West Virginia. Local jurisdiction was an issue. The jurisdiction issue eventually went to the US Supreme Court to settle those involved could be legally prosecuted.

Jake grew up on his father's farm. He and his siblings worked long, hard hours supporting the family. Jake was the youngest of his siblings. Jake went to school but stopped after the eighth grade. He continued to work on the farm but looked forward to the day he would leave.

A good athlete, Jake played baseball in the local league. When he turned seventeen, a Cincinnati Reds baseball scout watched Jake play in a game and encouraged him to try out with the team. Jake traveled to Cincinnati and tried out for the team. He did well and they offered him a minor league contract, but he decided against playing baseball and returned home. A baseball life on the road with low pay and away from home is not what he wanted.

World War II ended in August, 1945. Later that year, Jake turned eighteen. He decided to enlist in the US Army. He completed basic training and received orders for Germany to become part of the occupational forces. Since he had never left the state of West Virginia, he was excited to travel to Germany.

Jake never flew in an airplane. After a long train ride to New York, he boarded the aircraft to begin his flight to Germany. It took eighteen hours to arrive in Frankfurt, Germany after several stops.

The remnants of war were everywhere. Frankfurt was still in ruins. People looked everywhere for help. Some rebuilding started, but it was slow and deliberate. The situation was desperate for the German people and economy. The Marshall Plan was still a year away from helping Europe rebuild.

Jake enjoyed the fruits of being part of the occupational forces. The Germans were friendly and engaging. The women were always willing to date soldiers to gain financial and emotional support. Some were desperate enough to prostitute themselves to survive.

Jake continued to do well in the Army. Jake obtained the rank of Sergeant by 1948. He also received his General Educational Development diploma (GED) the same year.

All was well with Jake as he looked forward to the future.

# Chapter 9

## MARRIAGE

Jake and Anna continued to see each other for several months. They eventually fell in love. Jake was restricted to his Army base but made every effort to see Anna whenever he could.

Two years later, Anna found out she was pregnant. The year was 1950. She thought this was not possible after the brutal assault by the Soviets. She was wrong.

Anna shared the news with Jake. She also went into detail about her ordeal with the Soviet soldiers reluctantly and expectations of not having children. Jake told Anna he already suspected the brutality since he heard all the horror stories. He understood and told Anna it was in the past and the future is what is important.

Jake told Anna he was thrilled about having a child. He wanted to get married right away. Anna agreed to marry him.

Unfortunately, they discovered soldiers must apply with the US Government to marry German foreign nationals. Jake went to his superiors and asked for the documents to apply for marriage. He was informed the marriage would not be approved. His commanding officer told him the Allied countries just formed an international police unit called Interpol which had jurisdiction over all European countries. Their first charge was to vet all German citizens to assure they were no longer loyal to the Nazi regime or were not war criminals. It would take several years to clear those desiring to marry US soldiers.

Jake requested and received permission to leave post and reside outside the base with the general German population. He and Anna rented a small studio apartment waiting on the birth of their child. A few months later, Jake received orders to rotate back to the United States. He appealed the order, but the request was denied.

The day came for Jake to leave. He packed his bags telling Anna he would be back just as soon as the Army would allow. Anna was six months pregnant and not sure Jake would be willing to return or will be unable to return. She was missing him already.

The cab came to pick up Jake to take him to the airport. Anna escorted him to the cab.

As the driver loaded Jake's luggage in the cab, the driver turned to Anna and said, "Do you remember me?"

Anna started to have flashbacks to that horrible night in Dresden with the four Soviet soldiers. "I'm not sure," said Anna. "I remember your face but can't remember from where?"

"I'm Sergeant Mikhail Petrov," he exclaimed.

"Yes, I remember you! You saved my life in Dresden," she told him.

Anna turned to Jake and told him, "Mikhail risked his life to save me. I would not be here today if it were not for him."

Anna asked Mikhail, "How did you come to Frankfurt too?"

"I did not agree with Stalin's edict supporting the brutality of the German people, so I decided to go AWOL and escaped to Frankfurt. I have no family in Russia. My family was killed in Leningrad during the war. I have no regrets about leaving Russia, but my life here has been difficult. Being a Russian in Germany has been hard on me. Life has not been easy."

Mikhail also shared with Anna and Jake that he ran into the four former Soviet soldiers a few weeks ago that attacked her. They left the Soviet Union too, after the war looking for a better life. All four had jobs in Frankfurt and were living well. None of them were married.

Jake asked to speak with Mikhail in private. Anna went back to the apartment. Jake had a long conversation with Mikhail. Anna tried but could not hear what they were discussing, but she saw Jake hand Mikhail an envelope. Anna returned as Jake and Mikhail finished their conversation.

"What were you two discussing?" asked Anna.

"Nothing of interest," replied Jake.

Then, Anna asked Mikhail to wait a few minutes as she went back to her apartment. She returned shortly giving Mikhail $300. Anna told him, "This is all the money I have, but I will always be grateful for your courage."

Mikhail thanked Anna with tears in his eyes as he and Jake left for the airport. Jake thanked Mikhail, again, for what he did for Anna and hoped he could help him one day. He reminded Mikhail of his promise to Jake.

Mikhail told Jake, "I keep my promises. It will be taken care of."

Anna could no longer afford the apartment or continue to work. She remembered Mr. Hoffmeier and his wife, the delightful old couple that helped her and Monika escape from East Germany.

After several inquiries, she contacted him and described her plight. Mr. Hoffmeier told Anna there was plenty of room for her and the baby at the farm. He told her she was very welcome. Anna packed her belongings and found her way to the farm.

The Hoffmeiers were kind and took care of pregnant Anna. Anna enjoyed being at the farm in rural Germany, much different from city life in Dresden or Frankfurt. The mix of hardwood trees and open pastures with cattle was pleasing to her sight. The snow seemed so much brighter and exhilarating in winter. The air was refreshing in the spring with flowers displaying their brilliant colors.

On June 5, 1951, Joseph came into the world, a beautiful seven-pound boy with a head full of blond hair. Joseph became the new love of Anna's life. The Hoffmeiers were supportive and continued to take great care of Anna and now Joseph.

Some of Jake's letters found their way to Anna. He wrote of his difficulty attempting reassignment to Germany. He continued to request overseas duty to be part of the occupational forces.

Anna was reading the local paper when an article caught her eye regarding the murder of four former Soviet Union soldiers in downtown Frankfurt. They were shot at a great distance while together at a local park. The reason for the killing was unknown. It was speculated that it was linked to an extremist German group of former Nazis.

Included with the news article was printed pictures of the four former Soviets. Anna screamed when she saw the pictures. It was them—the four soldiers that brutalized her, her mother, and countless others in Dresden. She knew Mikhail did this, but why after all these years? She wondered if Jake had something to do with it.

Jake finally received permission to return to Germany in 1953. He flew to Frankfurt and found his way to the farm. When he arrived, he met his new son.

Anna confronted Jake with the article regarding the shooting of the four former Soviets in Frankfurt. She asked Jake if he had anything to do with the death of the Soviets. Jake exclaimed, "No. Absolutely not!" Anna accepted his word, but little did she know Jake conspired with Mikhail to have them eliminated. Jake rewarded Mikhail handsomely for his task.

A few weeks later, they thanked the Hoffmeiers and returned to Frankfurt in Army-sponsored living quarters. The following week, Jake told Anna to interview with Interpol to be registered and cleared of being a Nazi, allowing them to marry. They scheduled an appointment with local Interpol agents. The agents interviewed Anna and told her it would take a few months to verify the information to clear her.

Approximately three months later, she received notification of her clearance. Anna and Jake were married the following weekend. They were now eligible for government living quarters near Frankfurt but had to be interviewed by a senior officer for clearance first. The review was scheduled with Colonel Larry Blakely.

The following week, the Castles met with Colonel Blakely. Colonel Blakely spent two hours speaking with the Castles. He was impressed with Jake and formed an immediate bond with him. Colonel Blakely approved their application for government quarters. He also invited them to dinner at his house in Frankfurt. Jake agreed to come but told Colonel Blakely he had to bring his three-year-old son, Joseph.

"Not a problem," exclaimed Colonel Blakely. "We have a four-year-old daughter, Susie. He will enjoy playing with her."

Jake, Anna, and Joseph went to Blakely's house the following evening. Jack introduced his wife, Mary Louise, to Jake and Anna. Mary was employed by the military as an art teacher at the local military dependent school.

They all enjoyed the evening especially little Joseph and new-found friend, Susie. Susie and Joseph played together like a little sister and younger brother.

Jake and Anna maintained their friendship with the Blakelys over the following months, although the Army frowned upon a commissioned officer fraternizing with an enlisted soldier. The young friendship between Susie and Joseph also grew.

Jake, Anna, and Joseph moved into their new apartment and lived there two months until Jake received orders for Fort Dix, New Jersey. This made Anna happy because her great uncle Wilhelm, and his wife, Rose, lived in neighboring Philadelphia.

Anna studied the United States in school. She also heard all the stories from Jake on how good life was in the US. She was excited to move to and experience a new life in the United States.

# Chapter 10

# TROUBLESOME YEARS

Anna corresponded with Uncle Wilhelm and Rose prior to leaving Germany for Fort Dix, New Jersey. Wilhelm and Rose left Germany for the United States in 1933 as Hitler took control of the country. Wilhelm was a chef in Germany. He opened a restaurant specializing in German cuisine in Philadelphia. Philadelphia was home to a large imported German population. His restaurant was extremely popular and extremely successful.

Wilhelm and Rose lived in a row house in Philadelphia but also owned a summer home in Browns Mills, New Jersey, just outside the eastern gate of Fort Dix. They offered the cabin to Anna, Jake, and Joseph until they could locate a suitable place to live.

Anna, Jake, and Joseph flew to New York City where Wilhelm met them. They drove to the cabin in Browns Mills and settled in.

Browns Mills is a small, unincorporated community with a lake at its center. It is primarily a recreational retreat for residents of Philadelphia approximately forty-five minutes away. The cabin was nice but small, rustic, and crude. Unable to locate the toilet, Anna was introduced to the outhouse in the backyard, a new US experience.

Six weeks later, Jake found a nice two-bedroom 800 square foot, frame construction, rental house near town. The house was small but adequate for three although challenging in the winter months with the cold and snow typical for New Jersey.

Anna made her first trip to the Army Commissary located in Fort Dix where she saw her old childhood friend Monika, the streetwise girl from Dresden. They hugged so long store patrons became embarrassed as they watched them.

Their conversation was mixed in German and English drawing much attention from customers and employees. They discussed their lives since they parted ways in Frankfurt. Monika told Anna she also married a serviceman she met in Frankfurt, Joe Jankowski. The Army assigned him to Fort Dix too.

Monika told Anna she has two young daughters. "I named the oldest, Anna, after you. She is four years old. I want her to grow up and be like you. Unfortunately, she has a severe case of cerebral palsy. She cannot walk and has difficulty speaking. She needs constant care. Monika continued, "My younger daughter is Alexis. She is three years old. I hope she will grow up and be like me. I really wanted two girls. I want to watch them grow and be as close as we were. I hope their lives will be as adventurous and exciting as ours in Dresden."

Anna and Monika agreed to stay in touch, but Anna was not sure their friendship could survive Monika taking care of an invalid child. It was not like Monika to be tied down even with a needy daughter.

Several months into 1954, Anna read in the local paper that Monika's daughter, little Anna, had died. Monika was implicated in her death. Anna was not surprised. Anna knew Monika was a free spirit and she could not see her tied down taking care of an invalid child. Anna did not want to believe Monika had anything to do with her child's death but suspected she probably did.

Weeks later, Anna read in the local newspaper Monika was arrested for the death of her daughter. Her trial was pending. Monika was facing fifteen years or more in prison if convicted. Anna planned to attend the trial to give her moral support. Just before the trial, Anna was subpoenaed by the defense as a character witness.

The trial started a few months later. The prosecution presented their case. The autopsy revealed Monika's daughter died from ingesting ethyl-glycol or antifreeze. They matched the antifreeze to the same type stored in Monika's garage. Witnesses for the prosecution testified Monika was frustrated with the constant care of her daughter. Joe, her husband, was never home or helped in her care.

Monika's defense attorneys presented their case. They contended Monika consistently proclaimed throughout this ordeal that she had nothing to do with her daughter's death. She was consistent and never changed her story. The defense argued there was no physical evidence Monika induced her daughter to drink antifreeze. Monika opted not to testify.

Then the defense attorney called Anna to the stand.

"How long have you known Monika?"

"Since I was a young child," responded Anna. "She was and still is my best friend."

Anna spent hours outlining her relationship with Monika and their childhood friendship. She talked about the bombing in Dresden.

"Monika helped me, and my mother survive. Then, later, she helped me escape the horrors of the Soviets by fleeing to West Germany," Anna told the jury. "Monika saved my life."

The attorney asked Anna, "Do you believe Monika hurt her child?"

Anna looked at Monika and said, "No" although she knew it was a lie. Deep inside her being, Anna knew Monika killed her child.

Anna left the witness stand. Both attorneys made their summations. The jury retired to deliberate. They returned with their verdict in four hours—guilty as charged. The judge sentenced Monika to twenty-five years in prison.

A few days later, Anna went to visit Monika at the prison for the last time. Anna told Monika, "I will write to you while you are here. But I must ask you first—did you kill little Anna?"

Monika nodded her head yes crying and explained, "I was going crazy trying to live my life, take care of another child, and my husband too. Little Anna absorbed all my free time. She could not eat or go to the bathroom by herself. She was confined to a wheelchair. Her speech was limited. She had trouble communicating with other people. I lost my mind and wanted it to end. I am not even sure Joe is little Anna's father. I am deeply sorry for what I did. I believe all of this was my punishment for the life I lived in Dresden and the life I have lived since then."

"I will never understand why you did this, but I forgive you," Anna told Monika as she wept uncontrollably. "I will write to you and, hopefully, you will get out of here early and find a way to live a productive life."

Monika's husband, Joe, divorced her because of the trial and death of little Annie. He received full custody of their surviving daughter, Alexis.

Jake was introduced to Army football and baseball. Each military post sponsored their teams in football, basketball, and football, competing for the Army trophy each year. Many players were draftees from the professional leagues required to serve two years in the military.

Jake tried out for the Fort Dix football and baseball teams. He played fullback on the football team and catcher with the baseball team. The football team did well that year. Fort Dix beat Fort Campbell in the Army championship game in 1953.

Jake and his quarterback, Johnny, developed a friendship during the football season. Johnny was named the most valuable player of the game. After his Army service requirements were completed, he was drafted by the Pittsburgh Steelers but, later, was traded to the Baltimore Colts. He set numerous passing records while at Baltimore. Several years after his retirement, Johnny Unitas was voted into the National Football League's Hall of Fame.

Jake, now twenty-six years of age, was exposed to the vices typically associated with the military—drinking, gambling, and infidelity.

Jake came home several times intoxicated in addition to losing most of his paycheck gambling. Things got so bad he had to hunt rabbits to eat meat with their rice, the only side dish they had available and could afford.

Later, evidence of infidelity became an issue with lipstick and perfume on his clothing. Anna told him he was still an immature hillbilly from West Virginia. This was not a lifestyle she could endure.

Anna finally had enough of Jake's indiscretions. She confronted him with his improprieties. She threatened to move back to Germany and take Joseph with her. A violent argument ensued. He threatened her with sexual misconduct by having friends lie to keep Joseph here. Anna did not want to lose Joseph, so she decided to stay.

Eventually, things worked out between Jake and Anna. Jake gave up his vices and concentrated on his marriage.

In April 1954, their second son, Mathew, was born. Mathew was a stout, solid baby weighing in at ten pounds. The birth of their second son matured Jake. He became a responsible father and devoted husband.

One day, Anna's leg started to give her problems to the point she had trouble walking. She went to the Army's doctor at the dispensary. The doctor found her leg had an infection. An X-ray found a piece of metal causing the problem.

They scheduled surgery to remove the metal from her leg and address the infection. After surgery, the doctor showed Anna the metal piece removed from her leg. It was shrapnel from a bomb obviously from her time in Dresden, another painful memory from her past.

The Army gave transfer orders to Jake for Fort Stewart, Georgia, near Savannah, sometime mid-1956. The Army paid for moving their possessions while Jake, Anna and the boys loaded the car and made the trip traveling historic US Highway 1 to Fort Stewart in three days. They found a rental house in nearby Pembroke.

A few weeks after Jake and Anna moved into their house, a violent thunderstorm rolled in from the west. Three o'clock in the afternoon became like a dark, moonless night. Lightning was intense, popping and cracking everywhere.

Jake arrived home looking for Anna. He found her in their walk-in closet with the light on, curled in a fetal position. Anna told Jake the storm reminded her of the three nights in Dresden, the relentless bombing with the threat she would be killed any moment.

The storm passed. However, Anna would become stationed and isolated in the closet with each passing storm. She felt this was her punishment for surviving the Dresden bombings.

Jake told Anna it was time for her to apply for US citizenship. Anna agreed and studied the material provided for the test. She went to the US Courthouse in Savannah, took the test, and passed. She was given the oath and recited the Pledge of Allegiance. Anna was a US citizen.

In mid-1957, Anna and Jake's third son was born. They named him Kade. Kade was long, heavy, and born with flaming red hair. As the boys grew, they got along well. Celebrating Christmas was the most enjoyable time of the year for them.

Then in 1961, the boys' world was turned upside down.

# Chapter 11

# THE ACCIDENT

Anna continued to correspond with her mother in Dresden. She seemed to be doing well and in good health based on her letters. However, during August 1960, Anna received notice that her mother died. Her heart just gave away. Anna asked Jake for permission to attend her mother's funeral in Dresden. Jake encouraged her to go.

The next day, two agents from the Criminal Investigation Division of the US Army came to visit Anna and Jake. They were made aware of her mother's death. They informed Anna and Jake of the risks of traveling to East Germany in the current political environment.

The agents spoke with Anna about returning to Communist East Germany. They informed her a real threat existed of being detained as a citizen of Dresden, unable to return to the United States. The US Government would not be able to do anything to protect her or be able to return her to the States.

Anna thought long and hard about the risks of returning to Dresden. She decided to not go in the best interest of her boys and Jake. Anna cried for several days, not only for the loss of her mother but that she could not return home for her mother's funeral.

Anna and Jake were invited to a birthday party of a close friend of Jake's living in Savannah. They hired a babysitter for the boys before they started their journey to the party.

The party ended late in the evening, near midnight. It rained on the way home. The driver of a large tractor-trailer logging truck, fully loaded with logs, lost control, crossed the centerline of the highway, and hit Jake's car head-on. The Georgia Highway Patrol was dispatched to the scene along with an ambulance, but it was too late. Jake and Anna died instantaneously.

Soldiers at Fort Stewart took the lead in funeral preparations. They gave full military honors for Jake and Anna. Brigadier General Ray Stevens, Jake's former commanding officer in Europe, traveled from Washington, DC to attend the service and give the eulogy. General Stevens was on the Joint Chief of Staffs for the Army at the Pentagon. He spoke highly of Jake and Anna, how much in love they were with each other. "They were good, decent people."

Anna and Jake were buried together at a local cemetery in Savannah. All three boys attended but were unable to understand the reality of the tragedy. They were, however, emotionally overwhelmed by the loss of their parents. They became wards of the State of Georgia and placed in an orphanage near Savannah.

The boys made the best of their unfortunate situation, staying close to each other during their time at the orphanage. It was 1961. Joseph was ten years old, Mathew, seven, and Kade four. The head of the orphanage told Joseph they would make every effort to place them in a home together.

As time passed it became apparent no one was willing to take or adopt all three boys together. The orphanage finally decided to allow separate adoptions for each boy.

# Chapter 12

# KADE SMITH

Debbie and Al Smith came to the orphanage in Savannah early in 1962 looking for a boy to adopt. They were attracted to Kade. He was young and fit the profile of what they were looking for in age and characteristics. They adored his fiery red hair and blue eyes.

The orphanage investigated the Smiths. The Smiths were blue collar, lower middle-class citizens of a small community just north of Atlanta. Mr. Smith worked as a mechanic and his wife was a homemaker. They were found morally sound and capable of being good parents.

Kade met his new parents. Legal proceedings changed Kade's last name from Castle to Smith. Kade said goodbye to his brothers just prior to leaving in a very emotional send off.

Joseph told Kade, "I will find you one day, and we will be together again! I promise."

Joseph and Mathew wept uncontrollably as Kade drove away.

Kade had difficulty adjusting to his new life. Not only did he lose his parents, but he lost both of his brothers too. This had a long-term, subconscious impact on him. When Kade turned five years old, he became bitter and constantly challenged his new parents.

Kade had trouble making friends throughout his early school years. He often found himself in trouble, disciplined frequently when he fought or caused disruptions in class. Kade failed to apply himself in school. He was not a good student.

Debbie and Al were incredibly supportive of Kade, but as time passed, they started to question themselves on his adoption. During a heated argument, Al told Kade, "We wish we never adopted you!" This did not help Kade as he continued to spiral out of control.

Kade's high school years were troublesome. He became anti-social. He "hung out" with boys that were social outcasts. Kade was introduced to alcohol and drugs. His downward spiral continued.

Kade quit school during his senior year in 1975. Thanks to Al, he found a part-time job at a tire shop in the town of Emerson. He left Al and Debbie and moved in with some of his friends.

Unfortunately, the drugs and alcohol became his demon. He was eventually arrested for possession and sale of cocaine in 1976. He was convicted and committed to the county's prison to serve ten years.

As Kade sat in prison, he contemplated suicide. Al Shields, a prison guard, knew Kade was not in a good place mentally. For Kade, it could not get any worse.

"I'm a screwup, a lost soul with no sense of purpose, a drug user and now a convict with no hope for the future," said Kade. "My parents didn't deserve this."

Al told Kade, "I'm sad you're hurting. What can I do to help? Do not give up on yourself. Do not give up on hope. Life will get better. I promise."

They continued their conversation for two more hours. It inspired Kade to move forward and to have hope. Al saved Kade's life.

# Chapter 13

## MATT KENNEDY

James and Wanda Kennedy, a husband and wife team of pharmacists for Eckerd Drug Stores in Macon, Georgia, were unable to have children. They decided to adopt. They found the orphanage in Savannah and made an appointment to explore the possibility of adopting a child.

Staff members introduced them to various children. They focused on Joseph, ten years old at the time, older than most of the children being housed at the orphanage. They spoke with Joseph and found him to be bright and very polite.

Mrs. Kennedy asked Joseph, "How would you like to come home with us?"

Joseph, now called Joe, responded by saying, "That would be fine, ma'am, but I would prefer you consider my brother, Matt. He is much better than me. He would bring much joy to your life."

Shocked by the response, Mr. Kennedy asked Joe, "Is this what *you* want?"

"Yes, sir," responded Joe.

Mr. and Mrs. Kennedy visited with Matt. Matt was big for his age, stocky, solid—not fat.

When asked if he would like to come home with them, he said, "Yes, ma'amm. I would like that very much."

Mr. and Mrs. Kennedy adopted Matt. Matt traveled to Macon with his new parents as Matt Kennedy.

Matt, eight years old, adjusted well to life with the Kennedys. Matt was intelligent and did well in school. He was an exceptional student. Matt was well liked. He had an outgoing personality, and never met a stranger.

Matt was athletic too. He was encouraged by his adopted parents to play sports. As he entered high school in the fall of 1969, he had played baseball, basketball, and football previously in Junior High School. Matt entered tenth grade as a six-foot, two-inch, 210-pound quarterback. He easily became the varsity's quarterback, leading his team to the region title and a trip to the state's playoff. The team lost in the first round.

Matt grew to six foot four inches his junior year. His football team breezed through their scheduled opponents winning ten games with no losses. They won all their playoff games going undefeated and winning the state championship. Matt was voted All-State quarterback. Matt started to receive interest from various colleges for a potential football scholarship.

Matt continued to do well in school. He was an outstanding student poised to graduate in the top five percent of his class.

Matt's football team did not do as well his senior year winning eight games with two losses. However, the team made the playoffs winning all their games for a second consecutive state championship. He passed for over 4,000 yards. He was selected All-State for the second year in a row.

At six feet five inches tall, Matt received over fifty major football scholarship offers to various Division I universities around the country. It was a difficult decision, but eventually he decided to accept a football scholarship from Notre Dame after a visit from Head Coach Ara Parseghian. James and Wanda Kennedy supported the decision.

# Chapter 14

✦

# NOTRE DAME

Matt left Macon and traveled to South Bend, Indiana, to enroll at Notre Dame in the fall of 1973. The campus spanned 1,250 acres comprising around 170 impressive and beautiful buildings. Notre Dame's campus was consistently ranked and admired as one of the most beautiful university campuses in the United States and around the world. It was particularly noted for the Golden Dome, the Basilica and its stained-glass windows, the quads, the greenery, the Grotto, Touchdown Jesus, its statues, and museums.

The stadium was historic. Matt passed the statue of Knute Rockne, a legend of football greatness, on the way into the stadium. Rockne was revered as Notre Dame's all-time greatest coach. He felt comfortable, like being home.

Matt started at quarterback his junior year in the fall of 1975. At six foot five inches and 225 pounds with a cannon-like arm, he led the Fighting Irish to two winning seasons and consecutive bowl victories. He set many Notre Dame passing records.

While at practice, Matt met Rudy Ruettiger, a small, five foot six-inch-tall walk-on football player. There was something about him that impressed Matt. Rudy had more determination and drive than anyone on the team. Unfortunately, Matt did not believe he would make the varsity team or even play in a game.

Matt ran into Rudy at the dining hall. He sat next to him and started a conversation. Matt complimented him on his drive and determination at football practice. Rudy thanked him. Matt told Rudy about growing up in Macon, Georgia, playing high school football.

Matt and Rudy exchanged their life stories. Matt learned Rudy's real name was Daniel Ruettiger and that he was born and raised in Joliet, Illinois, the third of fourteen children. Rudy told Matt he did not excel scholastically in high school in part due to dyslexia. However, he excelled in football at Joliet Catholic High School where he played for locally famous coach, Gordie Gillespie.

Rudy also told Matt he joined the United States Navy after high school, serving as a yeoman on a communications command ship for two years. He returned to Joliet and worked in a power plant for two years. His lifelong dream was to attend Notre Dame. He applied to Notre Dame but was rejected because of his low high school grades.

"I enrolled and attended nearby Holy Cross College. After two years, in the fall of 1974, I was accepted as a student at Notre Dame on my fourth try. It was during his time studying at Holy Cross that I discovered I had dyslexia," explained Rudy. "I harbored a dream to play for the Notre Dame Fighting Irish football team, despite being undersized. Head coach Ara Parseghian encouraged walk-on players from the student body, so, I thought I'd give it a try."

Rudy earned a place on the Notre Dame scout team, a squad that helps the varsity team practice for games. Merv Johnson was the coach who was instrumental in keeping Rudy on as a scout-team player.

Matt and Rudy friendship blossomed. Matt helped Rudy study. Rudy told Matt, "I am about to give up on making the varsity team. I'm considering leaving school and going back home."

"Keep working hard on the football field as well as the classroom and good things will happen," Matt encouraged Rudy.

"I'm a senior now and this is my last chance to play in a game," exclaimed Rudy.

"Keep working hard and I will try to help make your dream come true."

The last home game of the regular season in 1975 was against Georgia Tech. Tech was in the way of Notre Dame being invited to a major bowl game.

Notre Dame coach Parseghian stepped down after the 1974 season. Former Green Bay Packers coach Dan Devine was named head coach.

Although Coach Devine felt Rudy did not exemplify a walk-on Notre Dame football player because he was small and slow, he encouraged him to continue. Rudy eventually decided not to practice and leave the team. Matt and one of Rudy's coworkers encouraged him to "see it through—you're close to the finish line." He returned to practice that afternoon, late, to his surprise to an ovation by his teammates.

Matt asked for a meeting with Coach Devine the day before the Georgia Tech game. Matt asked Coach Devine, "I would like for you to consider Rudy to dress out and have an opportunity to play in the game tomorrow."

"Let me think about it. I know Rudy has worked hard in practice and his effort has made us a better team. Let me discuss this with the coaches and I will let you know," responded Devine.

Later that evening, Coach Devine went to Matt's dormitory room. He agreed to let Rudy dress out. However, Devine told Matt, "Since it is a critical game, Rudy will probably not play."

"That would be okay as long as he can dress out in his uniform," responded Matt. "Please let him lead the team on the field," he asked Devine. "This is his dream. He earned the right. Rudy practiced for four years for this moment. His resolve and determination made us a better team. This was his goal. Having a player lead his team on the field just before the game starts is a long-standing Notre Dame tradition. This is all he wants."

Devine agreed.

Game day arrived and Rudy led the team out of the tunnel onto the field just prior to the start of the game. His teammates and fans clapped for him.

Rudy actually played for three plays: a kickoff, an incomplete pass, and on the third play (the game's final play), he sacked Georgia Tech quarterback Rudy Allen. He was carried off the field by his teammates following the game to the crowd's chant, "Rudy, Rudy, Rudy!"

Rudy was the first player in Notre Dame history to be carried off the field by his teammates. Notre Dame won easily 24-3. Georgia Tech fans did not understand why the Notre Dame fans were yelling "Rudy" since their quarterback's name was Rudy. They were confused. But not the Notre Dame fans. They all knew Rudy Ruettiger.

Matt and Rudy remained friends over the years. Rudy graduated from Notre Dame and became a motivational speaker after several years as a lobbyist.

Rudy's drive and determination served as an inspiration to his brothers. All the brothers enrolled in college and received degrees. Along with Rudy, they were the first generation in their family that received their degree.

# Chapter 15

# THE KENNEDY FOUNDATION

Matt was selected fifth in the first round of the 1977 NFL draft by the Atlanta Falcons. He signed a favorable contract with an exceptional signing bonus. He was thrilled to play professional football in his home state.

The amount of money was beyond his belief and expectations. Matt knew he had to be careful and invest it wisely. He called his best friend from college, Doug Little, an investment advisor and stockbroker with a major investment bank. Doug agreed to manage his money where he could play football and not worry about his finances.

The first year of being an Atlanta Falcon, Matt met Alexis Jankowski at a "meet and greet" function focused on introducing the Falcon players to the public. They dated and married the following year. Doug was his best man. Three beautiful healthy boys followed.

While dating, Alexis never discussed her parents other than to tell Matt her mother was dead, and her father abandoned her when she was a young child. Alexis did not want Matt to know how embarrassed she was of her mother had been convicted of murdering her older sister. She refused to discuss her family. She never realized her mother and Matt's biological mother were both German and lifelong friends.

Matt played seven years for the Falcons. He was an outstanding quarterback leading the Falcons to several winning seasons and the playoffs after the retirement of his predecessor, Steve Bartkowski. He was named All Pro for three of his seven playing years.

An accumulation of injuries forced Matt to retire early in 1984. Matt lived modestly for his income during his playing years. Concerned for his family's future, he met with Doug to discuss his current investments and future investment strategies.

Matt was pleased with his investment portfolio managed by Doug. Although Matt was risk averse, Doug suggested reinvesting in technology stocks. He felt breakthroughs in technology would produce long-term wealth.

Doug told Matt, "I recommend buying into two small upstart companies, Apple and Microsoft. I also recommend investing in a new home improvement company that just started in Atlanta. I met the owners, Bernie Marcus and Arthur Blank. I feel they are destined for greatness. The name of the company is Home Depot."

Matt trusted Doug and followed his suggestion.

Matt focused on his family for the next several years but did accept speaking engagements. He was sought frequently as a motivational speaker. It was at one of these speaking engagements in 1995 that he met Barry Carver. Barry asked to meet for a lunch to discuss one of his projects. Matt agreed.

Matt and Barry met for lunch. Barry told Matt he is a substance abuse counselor.

Barry explained to Matt, "Substance abuse is growing and out of control nationwide but it's worse in Atlanta. I would like for you to consider jointly sponsoring a foundation to help set up nonprofit clinics and other counselors in the area to help those that cannot help themselves with drug and alcohol addiction."

Matt observed drug and alcohol abuse by his teammates in the NFL. It ruined the lives of the players and their families. Help was not available for them. Matt agreed to help them and others suffering from addiction.

Matt's investment account paid off with the help of his stock appreciation in Apple, Microsoft, and Home Depot. His investment account swelled to over $100 million.

Matt initially funded the foundation with $20 million with the promise of more as needed. Matt and Barry built the clinics and hired counselors. They named the foundation the "Kennedy Helping Hands Foundation" and named the clinics the "Kennedy Helping Hands Clinics." Participants were not obligated to pay for services. Referrals came from local courts, counselors, judges, the Veterans Administration, and Veterans Hospital.

Alex Williams was hired as director, operated the programs, and oversaw the development of the clinics. Alex, a former professional football player and longtime friend of Matt, had his own problems with substance abuse. But he found his way after he was helped by many of his friends. Matt trusted Alex.

Matt was pleased with the progress of Helping Hands Clinics. They helped people with addiction problems. He felt satisfied knowing he helped others. He spent time in many of the clinics and encouraging others to reach their goals and be substance or alcohol free. He received numerous awards and recognition for his generosity.

Matt came home late one evening after spending time at the clinic. Alexis and the boys were asleep. He looked in on the boys as they slept and wondered about his brothers, where they were and what they were doing. He became emotional. Tears streamed down his cheeks, as he thought about the time together with his brothers and how he missed them growing to adulthood.

# Chapter 16

## JOSEPH MASON

Joseph, now called Joe by the staff and other orphaned children, was passed over for adoption several times during 1961 and 1962. Prospective parents wanted a younger child. Joe was just shy of eleven years old.

Reverend Jim Mason was the minister assigned to the orphanage for the spiritual needs of the children. He visited Joe several times attempting to uplift and encourage him. He was extremely impressed with the young boy.

Reverend Mason spoke with his wife about Joe and discussed the possibilities of adopting him. The Masons were older. Their children were grown adults. Reverend Mason felt he was led to help Joe. His wife agreed. They adopted him in the fall of 1962. Joe was now Joseph Mason of Savannah, Georgia.

Joe was very conscientious. He helped his adopted mother around the house. He was an outstanding student, extremely intelligent and bright. He made straight As all through his school years. He played and enjoyed sports but was just an average athlete.

After Joe finished his junior year in high school, he looked forward to his senior year. It was 1968. He had great concern over the current political environment and the issues that were ripping the country apart.

Joe followed current events on television and the local news-papers. He saw that the Tet Offensive in Vietnam changed and inten-sified the course of the war which divided the country. President Lyndon Johnson also chose not to run for re-election due to the Viet-nam war. Also, the USS Pueblo was seized by North Korea that in-creased tensions with the United States. Furthermore, Martin Luther King's assassination increased racial tensions that resulted in riots in 140 cities and Robert Kennedy was assassinated two months later in Los Angeles during a campaign trip. The Chicago Seven riots at the Democratic Convention and the Black Power salute at the Olympics in Mexico City further polarized our country. Joe was not sure our country would survive.

Joe graduated from high school with honors in 1969. He looked forward to college, but knew the military draft was a concern. Joe felt obligated to serve even though he could receive a college deferment. He remembered his biological father was career military and thought it was the right thing to do if he got drafted.

This was the second year of the armed forces lottery draft because of the political acceleration of the Vietnam conflict. The lottery was broadcast on television. A number was drawn for all birthdays in 1951. If the number assigned to your birthdate was anywhere from one to fifty, you must report for duty immediately. Numbers up to seventy were highly probable for induction too. Number 11 was selected and assigned to Joe's birthdate.

Joe reported to Fort Benning, Georgia, for basic training. Upon com-pletion, he was assigned to the 1st Cavalry Division and received or-ders for Vietnam shortly thereafter. Joe traveled to the West Coast where he flew to Hawaii, and then to Vietnam.

Joe arrived at Cam Ranh Bay, Vietnam. He met Billy Maddox, his bunk mate. Billy was a real southerner from Tennessee. He was a

bit of a hillbilly but extremely likeable. He spoke with a syrupy southern accent.

When evening came, Joe turned in for the night. As he lay down,
a stray Vietnamese bullet went through the tent. Three seconds
sooner, Joe would have been hit. The realization set in that he could
die in this Godforsaken country but felt God was with him and would
protect him.

Several weeks later, Joe was assigned to a search and rescue squad.
Another squad was late returning to camp from a scouting mission.
Joe's squad was assigned to locate them.

Approximately eight miles from camp, Joe's squad was deep in
the jungle walking down a narrow path. Trees, bamboo, and thick
vegetation congested the extremely narrow path. The rescue squad
hiked for two hours when they located what was left of the missing
eight soldiers.

It appeared the Viet Cong set up a hidden machine gun nest at
the end of the path. As the missing squad approached, the Viet Cong
opened fire. The soldiers reacted by jumping off to the side of the
path seeking cover. The Viet Cong hid bamboo spikes in the vegetation off the side of the path. When the soldiers dove into the thick
vegetation, they fell on the spikes, mortally wounding those that were
not shot. The survivors were eventually shot.

It was difficult for Joe to witness the aftermath of the slaughter
of his fellow soldiers, but he also had to endure what he saw of the
Viet Cong's brutality. The dead soldiers had their testicles and penises
cut off or removed, stuffed into their mouths even while some of them
were still alive. Their facial expression or "death mask" was something
he will never forget. Joe thought it may have been better they were
shot after this gruesome, horrible, and painful act. They bagged the
bodies and returned to camp.

Months went by with little action other than occasional mortar
and rocket fire landing near the base. An increase in the soldier population at Cam Ranh Bay discouraged the Viet Cong from taking any

major actions. However, there was an intense, surprise attack with mortar, rocket fire and machine guns. Everyone scrambled to take cover during this intense barrage.

Joe fell into a bomb crater but noticed one of his soldier comrades was wounded, left in the field, exposed to the mortar fire explosions. Joe crawled over to him. Shrapnel sliced open the fallen soldier's midsection. His intestines were protruding. The soldier was in intense pain.

The shelling continued, but Joe took the wounded soldier's intestines, stuffed them back into his body, told him to take his hands and press on the wound hard. Joe carried the wounded soldier to the hospital bunker, safe from the ongoing barrage. The medic told Joe the wounded soldier would survive thanks to his action. Joe inquired about his wound. The medic told Joe,

"Oh, we pushed his intestines back into his body and sewed him up. He will be okay but will have a severe case of constipation for several days."

Several days later, Joe was awarded the Bronze Star, recognized for saving the life of a fellow soldier.

Time passed with less action. Joe was looking forward to going home. Tennessee Billy and Joe became good friends during their time in Vietnam. Tennessee Billy's family owned a farm near Knoxville. Billy was a farmer. He raised cattle on the farm too. Billy's parents planned to retire upon his return from Vietnam. His parents looked forward for Billy's return to operate the farm.

Vietnamese children from the local village visited the soldiers in camp. The hungry children looked for food and gifts from the soldiers. Billy made friends with an eight-year-old Vietnamese child. He nicknamed her "Sunshine." The soldiers occasionally gave her a chocolate bar and spare rations.

Joe noticed Sunshine had arrived early one evening. Billy was having a discussion with two of his friends when Sunshine came over to the group and pulled on Billy's pants leg looking for a chocolate bar. Then, suddenly, Sunshine exploded and killed Billy along with two other soldiers. Sunshine was laced with explosives remotely detonated by the Viet Cong. None of Sunshine's remains were located.

Joe wrote a letter to Billy's parents in Tennessee telling them what happened and discussed how proud he was to be his friend.

Days later, Joe wrote to his parents, "This war is different—one we will not win."

Joe served his two years with the Army, returning home from Vietnam a changed man. He went from an eighteen-year-old naïve, immature teenager to a twenty-year-old seasoned, mature man. He was asked many times about his experiences in Vietnam but would not talk about it.

It was 1971. Joe did not know what he wanted to do after the Army. He lived at home for the next several months looking for answers, reliving the war in his nightmares. Although physically fine, he was psychologically traumatized from the horrors of war.

Joe spent much of his time watching television seeing discord in our country with Charles Manson and his female "family members" found guilty of the grisly murders of Sharon Tate, Leno and Rosemary LaBianca. The United States increased bombing of North Vietnam. He witnessed on television the attempted assassination of Presidential candidate, George Wallace. Then, President Nixon was investigated for potential wrongdoing or involvement in the break-in at the Democratic Party's Headquarters Office at the Watergate Building in Washington, DC.

Joe spoke with his father for many hours and days while he stayed home. He asked questions about his adoption, his brothers, and parents.

Reverend Jim told Joe, "I do not know much about your biological parents. Your brothers were adopted by good families, but I do not know where they are. Adoption records are sealed, and that information is not available. I do remember an unclaimed suitcase from your birth parents at the orphanage. Maybe one day you can claim it."

Reverend Jim convinced Joe to turn to God for answers. Reverend Jim helped him find God for peace and direction in his life. Joe felt the presence of God which lead him to attend seminary and become a minister.

Joe investigated several known seminaries in the Southeast. He settled on the McAfee School of Theology at Mercer University in Macon. Joe enrolled and began his studies. He received his degree in theology three years later in 1974.

While in seminary, Joe developed an interest in the homeless, especially those that served in Vietnam. He felt called to help those lost souls. He found the largest concentration of homeless veterans were in Los Angeles. After he told his father his plan, he left for Los Angeles. His father encouraged him to follow his heart and go.

Joe arrived and found the largest homeless shelter in Los Angeles. He found the director of the shelter, Mike Crum, and offered his services. Joe's help and spiritual influence were gladly accepted.

Joe worked well with the homeless. He was especially sensitive to the Vietnam veterans that endured the hardships of life after an unpopular, polarizing war. He provided both direction and spiritual help to those in need. He served many of the downtrodden and homeless in the soup lines. He got to know them personally. He shared his Vietnam experiences with them.

One day, director Crum went to Joe and told him how much he appreciated his work at the shelter. "I have a friend in the movie business," he told Joe. "He is an assistant director and invited me to see the filming called a "miniseries" titled *Rich Man, Poor Man*. This would be the first miniseries for television. It's a new concept. Would you be interested in going with me?"

"Yes," responded Joe. "It will be exciting to see a movie in production."

The following day, Mike and Joe arrived at the studio. Mike's friend, Jerry, greeted them and placed Joe next to one of the cameras. The story line for the movie had to do with two brothers and how their lives turned out so vastly different. Joe wondered about his brothers, where they were and what they were doing.

After the filming session, Jerry asked Mike and Joe if they would like to meet the cast. "Of course," they exclaimed.

Jerry introduced the leading cast members of the production to Mike and Joe—Ed Asner, Nick Nolte, Peter Straus, and Susan Blakely. They exchanged pleasantries.

When Joe spoke to Susan Blakely he inquired, "Your name sounds familiar. You look like someone I know from my past."

"Well, maybe we crossed paths many years ago. You do look familiar to me. Where are you from or where were you born?"

I'm from Georgia, but I was born near Frankfurt, Germany. My father was military," said Joe.

"Wow!" I was born in Frankfurt. My father was military too, stationed in Frankfurt…. I remember you now! We were incredibly young kids then. Our parents were friends."

"I thought I might have known you in a previous life, but I remember you as Susie. What a small world," said Joe.

"Yes, getting smaller every day," remarked Susan. "My name changed from Susie to Susan for this production. I must get back on the set. Give me your mailing address and I will write you."

"I'll give it to Jerry," responded Joe.

Joe and Mike left the studio and returned to the shelter amazed by the connection with Susan Blakely, an up-and-coming movie star.

The following year, Joe read in the newspaper Susan Blakely won the Golden Globe Award for Best Actress in a television series drama for *Rich Man, Poor Man*. Susan Blakely kept her promise and wrote Joe. They corresponded over the years catching up since their childhood. Joe enjoyed watching her movies in the years that followed—*The Towering Inferno*, *Report to the Commissioner*, *Capone*, *The Concorde-Airport '79*, and *Over the Top*.

Joe left Los Angeles after a year. He felt good about his service at the homeless shelter. He made and helped many friends. He returned to Georgia and joined his father's church as an associate pastor. His adopted father needed help as age slowed him down.

Several years later, Joe applied to join the North Georgia Conference of the United Methodist Church. He received approval and was ordained a Methodist minister. He was assigned to Trinity United Methodist Church in downtown Atlanta. He was named Associate Pastor and eventually became Senior Pastor.

Joe met Karen Ryan, one of his parishioners, at a church social. They dated for several months. Joe proposed marriage and Karen accepted. They married a year later on July 4th, 1980, and anniversary date Joe could remember. The following year, Karen gave birth to a healthy boy. They named him James after his adopted father who had died three years earlier.

Joe took a personal interest in the homeless in downtown Atlanta, especially those afflicted by alcohol and drug abuse. He spent much of his time ministering and counseling Atlanta's lost souls.

# Chapter 17

# HELPING HANDS CLINIC

Kade was paroled from prison early in 1981 after five years of incarceration. On the day he was released, fifty-two hostages were also released twenty minutes after President Reagan's inauguration as the 40th President of the United States. Kade went home to his parents in Emerson. He felt lost and did not know what to do with his life. Hopelessness was his constant friend.

Kade decided to move to Atlanta with some of his high school friends. They found an apartment in a less than desirable area of Atlanta. Kade had found a job as a waiter at Joe's Sports Bar and Grill in the Buckhead area of Atlanta.

Kade earned a living and thrived on generous tips from the restaurant patrons. Patrons liked him. He made friends with many of them. Unfortunately, some of his newfound friends eventually took him down a road he had traveled before.

Kade enjoyed life. The next ten years were good for Kade. He had many girlfriends but none he liked on a permanent basis. His prior history of drugs and jail were an obstacle to marriage or establishing a permanent relationship. He was hopeful there was someone out there for him.

Kade met up with some of his new friends late one night at a popular bar in Buckhead. They enjoyed the evening but Kade had too much to drink and became intoxicated. Unfortunately, after a few years and more drinking parties, Kade became an alcoholic.

One night in 1995, Kade returned to his apartment extremely intoxicated after a friend's gathering. On the way home, he slammed into another car. He was lucky. The driver of the other car was not seriously hurt.

The Atlanta police charged Kade with DUI and locked him up in the Fulton County jail. Kade called a friend to get help with an attorney.

Kade met with the attorney, Don Grissom. Grissom told him, "You are facing one year in jail and a large fine. However, there is an alternative. You could plead guilty and offer to enter a DUI sanctioned court program. You would have to see counselors, attend Alcoholics Anonymous, pay a fine and do community service. The program will last one year to eighteen months. If you complete the program, your fine will be dropped or lowered."

Kade appeared before the judge a few days later. He agreed to the DUI diversion program in lieu of jail time. The judge explained community service to him. He recommended volunteering with the Kennedy Helping Hands Clinics.

"Volunteering at the clinic will help you with your alcohol addiction. You will help others by reflecting on your experience while meeting your community service hours," he explained.

Kade agreed to the program.

The judge told Kade, "Look up Alex Williams, the director. He will help you."

Kade scheduled a meeting with Alex Williams the following week. They met at the downtown office of the Helping Hands Center. Alex gave an overview of the center and what they were trying to accomplish. He asked Kade to work with the attendees by listening to their stories and giving them advice. Kade agreed. Kade started the next day.

In 1997, Kade finished the DUI court diversion program. It took him eighteen months. Kade just turned forty years old. Part of the diversion program required attending a graduation ceremony along with other graduates. He must speak a few words to those that have not completed the program to fulfill his requirement for graduation.

Kade attended the graduation ceremony. There were thirty-five individuals present that had worked their way through the program. Most importantly, Kade's adoptive parents attended the ceremony.

Kade was not sure what he was to say when it was his turn. He was not comfortable speaking about his journey, but he did.

"I was a lost soul before I came here and became part of this program. I had no direction in my life. I turned to alcohol and drugs for answers. I was adopted at a young age and resented that I lost my parents to an automobile accident and my brothers to adoption. I am grateful for the love and support of my adoptive parents, but I was not a good son to them. This program changed my life thanks to the help of the counselors and others assigned to help me. I have found my soul and purpose in life. I feel good about myself. I encourage you to work hard, be on time to all scheduled appointments and let these people help you. I promise… it will make a difference in your life."

Kade's parents wept uncontrollably as they listened to his speech. They knew he was on the right road now to a productive life.

Kade left his job at the sports bar. He went to work at Ruth Chris Steakhouse. He needed to stay away from bars, alcohol, and certain friends.

Alex called Kade and asked to meet. They met in Alex's office at the center. Alex told Kade he was impressed with his time at the center and how he helped many of the participants. Alex offered Kade a position with the center as a nonlicensed counselor, an advisor. The salary offer was twice what he was making at the restaurant.

Kade said he enjoyed his time at the clinic and felt it gave him a sense of purpose that was missing in his life. He accepted Alex's offer. He started the following week.

A few months later, Alex asked Kade if he would like to meet the founder of the clinics, the one who started the Kennedy Helping Hands Foundation, Matt Kennedy.

"Is that Matt Kennedy, the professional football player that retired from the Atlanta Falcons?" Kade asked.

"Yes," said Alex.

"Of course, I would," said Kade enthusiastically.

Alex agreed to set up a meeting the next time Matt was in town.

A couple of weeks later Matt came by the center. He spoke briefly with Alex, then they went to Kade's office. Alex introduced Matt to Kade. They exchanged pleasantries.

Matt told Kade he heard great things about his work at the center and encouraged him to continue. He told Kade that he has a bright future with the foundation. Kade hesitated a moment. He was speechless.

Then he asked Matt before he left, "Have we met before? You look awfully familiar."

"I don't believe so." Matt replied. "You probably remember me from television or some of my promotions."

Kade said, "No. Maybe when we were much younger."

Matt replied, "Well, I'm from Macon. Where are you from?"

"Emerson, Georgia," replied Kade.

"Well, maybe we crossed paths somewhere," stated Matt.

"Maybe," replied Kade. "In any case, it is a pleasure to meet you."

Matt and Alex left Kade's office. After they left, Kade had this unusual feeling about Matt in the pit of his stomach. He was sure they had met before. He wrote it off as someone he met in a previous life.

# Chapter 18

# THE OLYMPICS

Joe was reassigned to an at-large position by the North Georgia Conference of the Methodist Church in 1990. He continued his work with the Atlanta homeless and those afflicted by drug and alcohol abuse. Many of them were war veterans. He accepted this position and made it his personal crusade. He worked tirelessly over the next ten years. He received many accolades, recognitions, and awards for his efforts.

During his assignment in Atlanta, Joe was approached by representatives from the Atlanta Mayor's office late in 1995. Atlanta was awarded the 1996 Olympics in 1990 by the International Olympic Committee Organizers. Organizers were concerned about the homeless and downtrodden street people of Atlanta during the Olympics. They asked Joe, on behalf of Mayor Campbell and the Olympic Committee, if he would help relocate these individuals to shelters and safe houses to provide a better image of Atlanta since they would be in the world spotlight. Joe agreed to help.

Joe spent the next six months working with various "street people" relocating them to shelters established by the City of Atlanta. He became well known to those involved with the organizers of the Olympics. He met one of the security guards while involved with the pre-game ceremonies, Richard Jewell.

Joe was invited to the opening ceremonies as Mayor Campbell's guest. He was also invited to the "Jack Mack and the Heart Attack" concert at Centennial Park. Although this was not his type of music, he wanted to be part of the celebration.

Joe went to Centennial Park for the concert. While there, he ran into Richard Jewell, his newfound friend. They spoke for a few minutes as Richard went on to monitor the crowd for potential problems and crowd control.

A few hours later, Joe saw Richard running through the crowd telling them to leave. Joe stopped Richard and asked what was going on?

"I discovered a backpack with three pipe bombs. Help me clear the crowd."

Joe started to leave the area asking people to leave quickly when he heard the explosion. People panicked and scattered.

Joe ran to the area of the explosion. He helped the people that were hurt. Unfortunately, two people died, one from a heart attack as a result of the explosion. The other person died from the shrapnel of the pipe bomb. The carnage and confusion of the explosion caused Joe to have flashbacks of his involvement in the Vietnam War.

Richard Jewell was hailed a hero for possibly saving over a hundred people from death or injury. Days later, Jewell was considered a suspect by the FBI. The FBI thoroughly and publicly searched his home twice, questioned his associates, investigated his background, and maintained 24-hour surveillance of him. Joe thought this preposterous and went to the FBI to let them know he did not believe Richard Jewell was responsible.

Despite never being charged, he underwent a "trial by media," which took a toll on his personal and professional life. The pressure began to ease only after Jewell's attorneys hired an ex-FBI agent to administer a polygraph, which Jewell passed.

Jewell was totally cleared when Eric Rudolph was linked to the bombing, eventually caught, and convicted.

Reverend Joseph Mason's efforts with the homeless and disadvantaged was noticed by Alex Williams, Director of the Kennedy Helping Hands Clinics. He contacted Joe and asked to meet. They met the following week.

Alex asked Joe if he would be interested in working with the clinic by providing spiritual help for those center participants in need. He agreed to spend three days a week and provide whatever was needed to help the participants.

Joe came to the clinic the following week. He met Kade. They chatted briefly and agreed to have lunch together one day. Kade found that Joe came from Savannah and his father was a minister. Joe had this deep feeling they had met before or that he knew Kade from a prior time. He shook it off and left with this unusual feeling in the pit of his stomach.

Joe worked with the participants at the clinic. He provided guidance and spiritual help as needed. A Vietnam war veteran came to Joe and asked if he remembered him. Joe indicated that he did not remember him. The veteran introduced himself—Dan York. Joe still did not remember him.

"You saved my life on the battlefield at Cam Ranh Bay," exclaimed Dan.

Joe then remembered. Joe apologized to Dan and told him, "I buried all those memories from that year in Vietnam."

"That is why I am at the clinic," responded York. "I turned to drugs and alcohol to dull the pain of those memories."

Joe told Dan, "I know it was painful bringing home those horrible memories, but you survived and appear to be doing well. If you had the strength to survive a life-threatening war, you have the strength to overcome the demons of alcohol and drugs."

Joe prayed with Dan—an inspiring prayer that lifted Dan.

Dan left the center a new man. He continued his battle with his demons—and won. It was the beginning of a productive life. Joe saved his life a second time.

# Chapter 19

# THE BANQUET

Matt's life was good. He was happily married with three wonderful boys, who were now grown adults and successful. Matt was financially secure, independent, and lived well in a nice home in Alpharetta, Georgia. Still he felt his life was incomplete. He had an emptiness about him which deepened his depression.

Despite all of Matt's successes, humanitarian gestures and generosity, he did not sleep well. He longed to know what happened to his brothers. His dreams sometimes turned into nightmares.

Over the years, Matt looked at his three boys and saw how happy they were. He reflected on how happy he was with his two brothers. Maybe, one day, he would find that happiness again.

James and Wanda Kennedy, his adopted parents, died a few years earlier. Much of Matt's history and background were lost with their death. Matt hoped to return to the orphanage to find information on his birth parents along with their background and history.

Kade continued to do well at the center. The year was 2009. Alex approached Kade and asked if he would like to be the new center director of the clinic. In his excitement he said yes. Kade was charged with running the day-to-day operations of the center and report to Alex as needed.

Alex said the foundation's annual banquet would be in a few weeks. He informed Kade that he would be sitting at the head table along with Matt Kennedy (co-founder), Barry Carver (co-founder), Reverend Joseph Mason, Atlanta Mayor Bill Campbell, and Rudy Ruettiger. Former President Jimmy Carter would also be present as a special guest.

Alex told Kade, "Rudy will be the guest speaker for the evening. He and Matt were friends and teammates at Notre Dame."

The Foundation Banquet was a special occasion this year as they celebrated their fifth anniversary of existence. The banquet attracted over 350 notable guests. It was also an annual fundraiser for the foundation and centers.

Alex, Matt, Barry, Joe, Kade, Mayor Campbell, President Carter, and Rudy settled into their respective seats at the head table. Reverend Joe Mason led off the banquet with an opening prayer.

After dinner was served, Alex started the program with an overview of the Kennedy Helping Hands Foundation. He introduced the guest speaker, Daniel "Rudy" Ruettiger.

Rudy spoke about his life and humble beginnings. "I played football in high school and wanted to play for Notre Dame. Although I was small for college football, I decided to walk-on and try to earn a spot on the team. My goal was to lead the team on the field for one game—and I did."

He spoke about goals and direction in life. "If you don't know where you are going, any road will get you there," he told the audience. "I was lucky. The definition of luck is when hard work crosses paths with opportunity. Set your goals, work hard, and never give up."

Rudy went on to say, "Sometimes you need encouragement on life's path when life becomes difficult. As I was considering giving up my dream at Notre Dame, Matt Kennedy stepped up with words of encouragement. It didn't surprise me to see him start this foundation to help and encourage those who needed it the most." Rudy spoke for twenty more minutes. He thanked Matt for the invitation and for the words of encouragement when he needed it the most.

Rudy concluded his presentation by telling the audience he had a surprise guest. He introduced Daniel York. "I will let Dan tell you more about himself rather than a formal introduction—so here he is, Mr. Daniel York." As he made his way to the podium, Joe, Matt, and Kade all knew him from the Foundation Center.

Daniel started by saying, "Today I consider myself the luckiest man on the face of this earth. I stole this from Lou Gehrig's speech at Yankee Stadium as he was dying from ALS. However, I have survived, cheating death twice, once in Vietnam and once on the streets of Atlanta. I was a young, naïve soldier almost blown apart by a mortar round when another brave soldier came to my rescue, carrying me off the battlefield under a barrage of mortar explosions and enemy gunfire to safety."

Daniel continued, "Years later, my life was saved again when a man from this clinic found me at my lowest point and close to suicide. The horror of my experience in Vietnam drove me to drugs and alcohol. He spoke to me and gave me hope. I gave up the drugs and alcohol. I turned my life around. I went to the Veterans Administration and found a job at one of their hospitals. Eventually, I graduated as a counselor, then sharing my experiences hoping to save lives of others like me—and I have.

"As a result of this experience, I have been asked to give the "Hero Award" to this person. So, I present the first annual Hero Award to Joseph Mason, Chaplin of the Kennedy Center and the man who saved my life—twice."

Joe was asked to come on the stage. He received a large plaque with his name inscribed. "I don't consider myself a hero. I just felt I was doing the right thing and, in many ways, doing God's work. In many ways, the Kennedy Center has saved and improved my life. I thank everyone responsible for this award. I thank Matt and all the people at the Kennedy Center for what they are doing. They are the real heroes." Joe returned to his table quite emotional and overjoyed. Joe and Kade were inspired by Rudy's presentation. They had a much deeper respect for Matt and his accomplishments after his football career.

Matt approached Joe and Kade at the conclusion of the banquet and asked them, "I would like to invite both of you to dinner at my house in two weeks. Alex and Barry will be there too."

Joe and Kade expressed their gratitude for the invitation and told Matt they would be there.

Before leaving, Kade was approached by one of President Carter's security guards. "Kade—do you remember me?"

Kade looked at him and responded, "You look familiar. I should know you. Your face is familiar, but I cannot remember who you are. Please forgive me."

"My name is Al Shields. I was a prison guard once. You were an inmate under my supervision in 1976. Mentally, you were not in a good place, but I thought you were a good person having a tough time. Obviously, I was right. Look where you are now."

"Yes, Al," said Kade with his eyes beginning to tear. "If it were not for you, I would not be here today. You saved my life and I thank you."

"Well, I don't believe that. What I believe is not only did you save your own life but the lives of many others."

"Thanks, again," responded Kade.

"Let me introduce you to President Carter," said Al. "He knows a lot about you and the Center."

They moved over to President Carter's table. Al introduced Kade to President Carter.

"I am honored to meet you, President Carter."

"Well, I am honored to meet you too. You do as much for those in need in Atlanta as I do through Habitat for Humanity. Keep up the good work. I am sure we will meet again."

Kade left refreshed and energized.

# Chapter 20

# THE REUNION

Joe arrived at Matt's home shortly after Kade. Alex and Barry were already there. They chatted for a while before dinner.

The conversation continued after dinner. Matt revealed that he invited them to dinner in appreciation for their contributions to the Center. During the conversation, Matt asked Joe where he was from.

"Savannah. I had lived there since I was ten. I graduated from high school there too—then I was drafted. I had a college deferment but felt it important to serve our country. I had vague memories of my father being in the military. It helped me make that decision. I served two years in the Army, one of those years in Vietnam. I came home and then entered seminary school in Macon."

"Interesting," said Matt. "I'm from Macon. My parents were pharmacists for Eckerd Drug Stores. They were good to me even though I was adopted. They encouraged me to participate in sports for which I am forever grateful. They have since died."

"I'm sorry to hear of their passing," said Joe. "I'm sure they were great parents. By the way, I was adopted too."

Kade jumped in, "Funny—I was adopted too."

"Where are you from, Kade?" asked Matt.

"Emerson, Georgia. My parents adopted me when I was four. I don't remember much about the adoption or my birth parents other than they were killed in an automobile accident."

"That's incredible. My birth parents died in an automobile accident too," said Matt.

"So, did mine!" exclaimed Joe.

It was at that exact moment Joe, Matt, and Kade looked at each other and realized they were brothers, lost after the horror of their parents' death, that forever changed their lives and future. They stood up, came together in an enduring hug with indescribable tears of joy—and of sadness for all the years lost as brothers.

The evening was late. Alex and Barry left earlier, both happy for Joe, Matt, and Kade. The boys agreed to meet for dinner the following week and catch up on the past forty-nine years. Kade suggested Ruth Chris Steakhouse since he had connections. Matt and Joe agreed.

Joe, Matt, and Kade went to bed that night filled with excitement and joy. They could not sleep. None of them were this excited since they were adopted forty-nine years ago. They could not wait to be together again. Matt's dream came true and prayers were answered.

The following week the brothers met at Ruth Chris Steakhouse. They spent hours as they talked and caught up on their lives since their adoption in 1961. They were still engaged in conversation when asked to leave the restaurant. The restaurant closed at 11:00 p.m.

Most of their conversation centered around their biological parents. None of them knew much about them. Even though Joe's adoptive father was the minister at the orphanage, he knew little of their biological parents other than they were killed in a horrible accident. He did tell Joe that his father was in the military, and his mother was of German descent but that was all he knew. Joe vaguely remembered them.

Joe remembered his adopted father told him about a suitcase left at the orphanage after the accident. His father found it at the house after the funeral and did not know what to do with it. The orphanage hoped a relative would eventually claim it. Joe thought it might still be at the orphanage.

The brothers mutually agreed to find out as much information as they could about their biological parents to understand their heritage and learn more about their parents' lives. They planned to start with a visit to the cemetery and then follow up on the suitcase.

# Chapter 21

# THE SUITCASE

The brothers decided to find the graves of their parents. Joe called the commanding officer at Fort Stewart to see if they had any information on the location of their parents' grave sites. He referred them to an officer in another area of the base. The new officer located the information the brothers were looking for and passed it on to Joe. Sgt. Jake Castle and his wife, Anna, were buried at Happy Hill Cemetery in Savannah.

Joe offered to drive to Savannah. Matt and Kade agreed. After the five-hour trip from Atlanta to Savannah, they located the cemetery. They located their parents' graves, paid their respect, and left for the orphanage.

Joe agreed to be the spokesperson at the orphanage in the event there was a privacy issue. He felt his adoptive father's years of service at the orphanage would be worth some consideration.

They drove to the orphanage. He had scheduled an appointment with director Hal Wright. Joe told the story about him and his two brothers that were adopted from the orphanage in the early '60s. Joe explained that they sought information on their biological parents.

Hal told Joe, "I don't know anything about your parents. We do not keep information on the biological parents, just the adopting parents for legal reasons."

"I was told about a suitcase held for the nearest relative of Sgt. and Mrs. Castle," said Joe. "Is it still here unclaimed?"

"I don't know, but I will check. We have a storage facility on the grounds. If we have it, it will be there."

Hal returned after about forty-five minutes with the suitcase. Joe signed a release that he acknowledged he was the nearest living surviving relative. He left and carried the suitcase like it contained a million dollars. To Joe, it was worth more than that.

The brothers decided to wait until they returned to Atlanta to examine the contents of the suitcase. They agreed to meet at Matt's house the following evening.

Joe and Kade arrived at Matt's home the next day. Matt kept the suitcase unopened. He placed it in the middle of the living room floor in front of the fireplace.

Matt's boys were invited to attend. Matt introduced his newfound brothers to his sons as "Uncle Joe and Uncle Kade." Matt introduced his sons, "Peter is thirty-two years old, married to Sally and is an Atlanta lawyer but is working as an aide with US Senator Johnny Isakson. He aspires to run for public office one day. John is thirty years old, married to Mary, and is the head football coach at Bear Creek High School in Atlanta. He is also a former outstanding football player at Georgia Tech. He hopes to move into coaching in the college ranks someday. James is twenty-seven years old. He has not found the love of his life yet. He is Vice President with Bank of America in their corporate banking division in Atlanta. He hopes to start a new bank one day and operate it as the bank's President and CEO."

The brothers interacted with Matt's boys for over an hour. They caught up on their lives, learned of their interests and goals for the future.

The brothers and Matt's boys gathered in the living room to open the suitcase. The suitcase was old, worn out, dirty, and dusty. The locks were rusted. Matt easily broke the locks, opened it and revealed the contents.

The suitcase was full of papers and pictures obviously that belonged to Jake and Anna, collected over their lifetime. Joe found original birth certificates—first Anna's and then Jake's. Anna's birth certificate was German from a hospital in Dresden, Germany. Jake's was from Williamson, West Virginia.

Joe found Matt's and Kade's birth certificates. They were certified copies but not the originals.

Then Joe found his birth certificates—two of them—one in German and one US issued. He assumed this was normal since he was born in Germany and his father a US soldier. But as he read the German issued birth certificate, his last name was listed as his mother's maiden name, Schmidt. He was puzzled.

Matt found Anna and Jake's marriage certificate. It was dated in 1953. The boys were confused because Joe was born in 1951. Again, more questions with no answers.

Kade found Anna's immunization records from the 1930s, school report cards, work permits, naturalization papers, Interpol investigation reports and a clearance letter. He also found a picture of a young Anna as she shook hands with Adolf Hitler. There were many other pictures of Anna and Jake together, many which showed how much they were in love.

As they rummaged through the suitcase, Matt found what seemed to be a hundred letters, mostly addressed to Anna. The boys made a list of all the senders. It included Monika Jankowski, Mrs. Hoffmeier, Colonel Ray Stevens, Anna's mother - Ingrid, Uncle Wilhelm and his wife Rose, and Mikhail Petrov. Additionally, there were several letters sent to Jake and Anna from Jake's family in West Virginia. The most intriguing find was the detailed diary written by their mother from early in her life to her days in Frankfurt.

"Monika Jankowski" said Matt. "Jankowski is my wife's maiden name. What a coincidence."

Matt suggested they split the letters up, take notes and discuss later. They read the numerous letters and Anna's diary the rest of the evening. A picture developed on who their parents were and much about their lives until their untimely death in 1961.

A few weeks later Joe, Matt, and Kade met for lunch to discuss what they found in the letters. It took weeks for them to digest the letters' contents. Many questions were answered but there were still many unanswered questions which generated much confusion.

"We need to find out more about our parents and our early years," stated Matt. "Knowledge of our heritage and parents are paramount to knowing who we are, not only for us but, for our children and grandchildren."

"I agree," said Joe. "We need to get answers to our questions. The best way is to contact the writers of these letters and seek answers."

Kade asked, "Who or where do we start?"

"Monika was her best friend, not only during her childhood but her early adult years," said Joe.

"Let us start with her. I will see if I can find her from these letters. Hopefully, she is still alive. Her last known address was in Mount Holly, New Jersey. With the last name of Jankowski, she shouldn't be too hard to find."

"Yes, but Monika was serving time for killing her daughter," said Matt. "Hopefully, she is out of prison and still alive."

Matt told his brothers he would search West Virginia for Jake's family. The letters referred to three brothers—Ernest, Cecil, and Loren. Matt will attempt to contact one of them and arrange a visit.

Joe found Monika. She still lived at the same address in Mount Holly, New Jersey. Joe called her and explained who he was—Anna's first-born son. This was quite a surprise for Monika. They spoke briefly before Joe asked if he and his brothers could visit her sometime during the next few weeks. She agreed.

Joe shared the news with his brothers. They agreed to leave for New Jersey in two weeks.

Joe, Matt, and Kade flew to Philadelphia and made the short road trip to Mount Holly. They found and met with eighty-two-year-old Monika. She was in poor health, but her mind was clear.

"We are here to learn about our mother and father. We found some of your letters to Anna, our mother. We have a lot of questions about her. We want to know who she was. We lost her and our father when we were young. Can you help us?" asked Joe.

"I will try," said Monika.

Monika talked about Anna for over three hours. She described to the boys what kind of child she was as she grew into adulthood. "I was proud to call her a friend," exclaimed Monika.

She explained about the horrors of Dresden—being bombed, Russians, the escape to West Germany, when she met their father, Jake.

Monika explained, "In later years, things got difficult with my handicapped child, then her death. We stopped writing to each other shortly after that—and I knew why. But I still loved and revered your mother. She was a wonderful person. Anna told me that she wanted to be more like me, supposedly brave and bold. The truth is, I wanted to be more like her."

Joe asked Monika about his birth certificates.

Monika explained, "We all lived in Germany at a time when none of the Americans trusted Germans after the war. Many German girls fell in love with Army servicemen. They wanted to get married but could not until they were cleared by Interpol. By then, many children were born. German birth certificates were issued. When mothers were cleared by Interpol later, a US birth certificate was issued naming the father. This was quite common. My husband and I did not marry right away. We had a daughter before we were officially married. We eventually married and moved to New Jersey where he left the Army. Unfortunately, my husband divorced me after the death of our oldest daughter."

Joe said with a sigh of relief, "Well, that explains my two birth certificates. One mystery solved."

Matt asked Monika, "Did you know Uncle Wilhelm and Rose?"

"Yes, I met them. Good people and they loved Anna. They left Germany for the States before the war. They did well and had money. They gave Anna some money to help her on her trip to Georgia."

"Jankowski is my wife's maiden name," Matt told Monika.

Monika asked, "What is her first name?"

"Alexis," Matt responded.

Monika smiled and told Matt, "That's my daughter. I heard she married a famous football player. You are my son-in-law."

Matt was speechless—in shock. Eventually he told Monika that Alexis never spoke of her mother and that her mother was dead.

"I can understand why she never spoke of me," stated Monika. "I was convicted of killing her older, disabled sister. They ruled it murder, but it was an accident. I hope she will forgive me one day."

The brothers finished their conversation with Monika and thanked her as they left.

On the way back to Atlanta, they realized how fortunate their mother was to survive all the horrors of Dresden but were encouraged how brave and resilient she was as she escaped East Germany for a better life.

# Chapter 22

# WEST VIRGINIA

Most of the questions about the boy's biological mother, Anna, were answered. But they did not know much about their father, Jake.

The brothers decided to review the letters from Jake's family. They found Jake had three brothers. Kade agreed to take the lead on locating one or more of Jake's brothers.

Kade's research found one of Jake's brothers, Ernest. Kade found him just outside Williamson, West Virginia. Kade called him to see if he and his brothers could visit. They let him know they were his long-lost nephews. Ernest agreed. They set a date for the visit.

The brothers flew to Huntington, West Virginia, rented a car and drove to Williamson. It was the year 2011. They found Ernest at the farm his father previously owned. Ernest greeted the brothers and introduced Loren, Ernest's brother. Ernest told them he inherited the farm upon his father's death. He remained a farmer because "That's all I know."

Ernest told the brothers, "My older brother, Cecil, died several years ago from Black Lung Disease. He was a lifelong coal miner.

Here in rural West Virginia, you farm or work in the coal mines or grow marijuana. Coal mining was his choice. Farming was my choice—but not marijuana (laughing)."

They entered the farmhouse and sat at the kitchen table. Ernest and his wife, Mary, prepared a farm-fresh lunch. The brothers watched the preparation of the meal as Mary beheaded a hen, pulled corn off the stalk, and pulled potatoes from the ground, served with fresh milk from their cow. They never had a better meal.

They spent hours learning about their father, Jake. They discovered their heritage and connection to Devil Anse, a nickname for Asa Harmon Hatfield of The Hatfields and McCoys infamous feud. Ernest spoke of Jake's athletic ability.

"Now I know where I got my athletic abilities," exclaimed Matt.

Ernest was home when Jake announced to his parents he joined the Army.

"Our parents were opposed to it," said Ernest. "But I supported him because he would never be happy with a life in West Virginia. Through his letters, I know he found happiness, especially with Anna. He made the right decision. He was madly in love with Anna."

The brothers were delighted to hear that.

The circle was complete now that they met their uncles, nephews, and nieces. They felt whole for the first time in their lives. They understood their humble beginnings and simplicity of their father's life in the mountains of southern West Virginia as they returned to Atlanta.

In the weeks that followed, the brothers discussed everything they found out about their parents. They felt one more task was needed to complete their fact-finding mission.

"We need to travel to Dresden for no other reason than to understand our mother's background and visit the castle-apartment on the Elbe River where she grew up," stated Joe.

The brothers agreed.

Three months later, the brothers packed their bags and flew to Dresden by way of Berlin. They were met by their personal guide, Bern. Bern was older and spoke good English. His grandparents were survivors of the Dresden bombing.

They toured Dresden. Bern was excellent as he pointed out historical sites throughout the city. He had many "before" and "after" pictures of Dresden from the war.

They located the castle on the Elbe River. It was converted to a museum. The boys felt the presence of their mother as they walked through the structure. They tried to imagine where their mother hid during the bombings. They understood how she survived but were still amazed that she made it.

Joe asked Bern if he was familiar with the town of Meiningen.

"I am," replied Bern.

"We would like to find the Hoffmeier Farm. If we paid you, would you drive us there?"

"Of course."

They left Dresden and drove to Meiningen. Once they arrived, Bern asked some of the locals if they knew the location of the Hoffmeier Farm. He got directions. They left and drove to the farm.

Once at the farm, they saw a young man outside the farmhouse. Bern and the brothers approached him. Bern asked, in German, if this was the Hoffmeier Farm.

"Ja ist es (Yes, it is.) Wie kann ich din helfen (How can I help you?")

Matt asked, "Do you speak English?"

"Yes, I do," he replied in English. "My name is Hansel Hoffmeier."

"We are looking for Mr. and Mrs. Hoffmeier, an older couple, that took care of our mother, Anna Schmidt, right after the war."

"They were my grandparents. I remember them speaking of Anna and Monika with great fondness. They liked the young girls. Anna came back later with a young son and stayed for a short time."

"That son was me," said Joe.

"That is unbelievable," exclaimed Hansel. "It is a pleasure to meet you."

Matt told Hansel they came to Germany to find out more about their mother's early years. He told Hansel of her untimely death and of his subsequent adoption.

Hansel invited them to eat dinner with him and his family. They spent the evening as they shared their stories. The boys learned more of their mother's early life.

Bern took them to the Frankfurt Airport late that evening for their return trip to Atlanta.

# Chapter 23

# PRESIDENT KENNEDY

Life returned to normal for the brothers in the years that followed. The year is 2022. The brothers and their families have the joy celebrating Christmas together as a family. They continued to talk about Anna and Jake and the challenged life they had. All three brothers wished their parents were still here to enjoy the families and to see how well they turned out.

Joe continued his work with the homeless and downtrodden in Atlanta. He had a successful marriage. His son, Paul, followed in his father's footsteps and became a minister.

Matt continued his involvement in the Kennedy Helping Hands Foundation and the clinics. His outreach program expanded to seven major cities. His wealth allowed him to continue his role as a philanthropist as he donated to many just causes.

Kade continued his work with the Kennedy Helping Hand Centers. He became the Executive Director for the organization. Kade finally found the love of his life and married in 2012. He and his wife were too old to have children. He often thought that his late marriage with no children was the price for his sins of his past.

Matt's son, Peter, continued as a lawyer but announced his candidacy for Governor of the State of Georgia on the Republican ticket.

Matt and the family agreed to support him. Matt's other son, John, left his coaching job at Bear Creek High School and became the Offensive Coordinator/Assistant Head Coach at Georgia Tech.

And last, James, reached his goal and started a newly chartered bank. He helped raise $100 million for startup capital. Of course, Matt was a significant investor. James was elected President and CEO of the bank.

Peter Kennedy had an active campaign. His opponent, Tracy Abraham, was well liked especially with minorities. She was a formidable opponent. Former President Jimmy Carter, now ninety-seven years old, although a Democrat, supported Peter.

Peter was elected and became Governor Peter Kennedy in an extremely close race.

Kennedy's term was productive and generally accepted as successful. He accomplished great things for Georgia. Georgia was recognized as one of the more progressive states in the union during his term.

Four years after his election, as his term as Governor ended, Peter announced his candidacy for President of the United States. His announcement was widely supported by the Republican Party.

Candidate Kennedy came through the Republican primaries relatively unscathed. However, that was not always the case in the debates with the Democratic incumbent and the media. The press printed articles about Candidate Kennedy's grandmother, branding her a Nazi war criminal and spy. He was also questioned about being related to the notorious Devil Anse of the Hatfield family.

Peter survived all the implications and lies and received the party's nomination. He was elected 47th President of the United States in 2028.

President Kennedy attended the funeral of a lady unknown to the press and a relatively unknown person even in her community in New Jersey. Monika Jankowski died at the age of 101. Joe, Matt, Kade, and President Kennedy's sons attended.

Matt's wife, Alexis—Monika's daughter and only surviving family member—also attended. She cried uncontrollably during the funeral. She felt guilty of not having seen her mother or re-established their relationship especially after she heard the stories of Anna, Matt's mother.

President Kennedy was asked by the press after the funeral, "Who was this woman?"

President Kennedy addressed the press in a manner honoring a fallen soldier or dignitary, "Monika Jankowski is my hero. She convinced and helped my grandmother escape Communist occupied East Germany in 1946. Monika was smart and brave. My grandmother was her best friend. My grandmother would not have attempted this incredibly dangerous escape on her own. If it were not for Monika, I would not be here today."

President Kennedy concluded saying, "Let us all learn a lesson from Monika. Be kind to others, be determined, be smart and never give up. I honor her today for her life and what she meant to our family."

President Kennedy thought it not in his best political interest to disclose Monika was his wife's mother. Issues about the death of her child and subsequent conviction would surface a lot of pain in the family in addition to forming a cloud over his presidency.

President Kennedy returned to the White House. Joe, Kade, and the Kennedy brothers returned to Atlanta.

# Chapter 24

# BROTHERS

The Castle brothers enjoyed a different Christmas in the White House with President Kennedy. Celebrating Christmas had special meaning, not because it was held in the White House but because of their beginnings and heritage. The sons and grandsons of a West Virginia hillbilly and a German Nazi that survived the war and the Soviets ultimately produced the President of the United States.

Santa Claus came to the White House this year in his shiny red suit, real white beard, and white hair. He had gifts for all the White House staff's children and the others that attended. President Kennedy and his brothers also in attended.

"Ho, ho, ho. Merry Christmas!" yelled Santa as he passed out gifts. "I have a special gift for Rev. Joe Mason. Is he here?"

"I am," said Joe.

"Well, I have a special gift for you. Here, in this package."

Joe took the package and opened it. In a box he found a gold watch. On the back was the inscription that read, "This gift in gratitude for the man that saved my life twice – Dan York."

Joe looked up at Santa Claus and smiled. He realized Santa was Dan York. Santa "winked" at him as he left the White House. Later, Joe discovered Dan worked with children at St. Jude Children's

Hospital in Memphis, Tennessee, as a skilled nurse. At Christmas time, he played Santa Claus.

The Castle brothers spent much of their time together these days as they reflected on their parents. They hoped their children and grandchildren would appreciate the trials and tribulations of their grandparents, Anna and Jake.

It took almost fifty years for Joe, Matt, and Kade to find each other after that terrible accident and their adoption. They spent much time together since their discovery and made up for their lost time.

Joe, Matt, and Kade came through the death and destruction of the Dresden bombing by way of their mother, Anna Schmidt Castle. Anna came out of the fire and ash of Dresden in February 1945, and delivered three, wonderful and productive sons. Of course, her grandson became President of the United States.

They are the "Castle Brothers." A synonym for Castle is "Stronghold" or "a place of security or survival." How appropriate.

President Kennedy ran for a second term in 2032 and won. Joe, Matt, and Kade are now in their seventies and eighties. But life would change for the Castle brothers as grandchildren have not always followed in the righteous footsteps of their parents or grandparents.